A

14 MAY 14

18. JUL 14

29. 10. 14

17. SEP 15

22 FEB 18

13. JUN 16

NORFOLK LIBRARY
AND INFORMATION SERVICE

Dear Reader,

I've often wondered how a person with a genetic urge to seek excitement managed their life. In some ways, I was able to satisfy my curiosity while writing Zach's story… because Zach Coulter has a lifelong history of pushing the boundaries, testing the outer limits of his endurance and chancing death whenever possible. His mother, Melanie, also possessed a reckless nature—and when the eleven-year-old Zach dared her, Melanie had jumped into the creek to join him—and died.

Twenty-three years later, Zach returns to the Triple C, where—he's always believed—he caused his mother's death. He plans to stay in Montana only long enough to join forces with his brothers and save the ranch they've all inherited. But the world shifts on its axis when he meets and joins forces with beautiful Cynthia Deacons. Soon, he begins to wonder if Cyn might permanently satisfy his thirst for excitement and calm his restless heart.

I hope you enjoy reading Zach Coulter's story and that you'll return with me soon to the Triple C Ranch and the third installment in Big Sky Brothers when Zach and Cade welcome home the youngest, famed silversmith Eli Coulter.

Warmly,

Lois

THE VIRGIN AND ZACH COULTER

BY
LOIS FAYE DYER

MILLS & BOON

First published in Great Britain 2012
by Mills & Boon, an imprint of Harlequin (UK) Limited,
Eton House, 18-24 Paradise Road, Richmond, Surrey TW9 1SR

© Lois Faye Dyer 2011

ISBN: 978 0 263 89483 7
ebook ISBN: 978 1 408 97868 9

23-1112

Harlequin (UK) policy is to use papers that are natural, renewable and recyclable products and made from wood grown in sustainable forests. The logging and manufacturing processes conform to the legal environmental regulations of the country of origin.

Printed and bound in Spain
by Blackprint CPI, Barcelona

Lois Faye Dyer lives in a small town on the shore of beautiful Puget Sound in the Pacific Northwest with her two eccentric and lovable cats, Chloe and Evie. She loves to hear from readers. You can write to her c/o Paperbacks Plus, 1618 Bay Street, Port Orchard, WA 98366, USA. Visit her on the web at www.LoisDyer.com.

For my sister Shirley—
children need more extraordinary schoolteachers
like you

Prologue

"Hey, Zach, the phone's for you!"

Zach Coulter laid his cards facedown on the down-filled sleeping bag and stood. Outside the sturdy tent, the wind moaned and tugged at the corners and tie-lines while a half-moon cast silver light and shadows over the Mount Everest base camp.

"Don't look at my cards," he warned his two companions, grinning at their four-letter-word responses as he crossed the tent and took the satellite receiver from the team leader. "Hello?"

"Zach, it's Angela."

"What's up? Everything okay?" Zach tensed, a frown creasing his forehead.

Static crackled on the line, but then his assistant reassured him with her usual crisp, no-nonsense tone. "Your brother Cade has been calling. I told him you weren't reachable until you descended to base camp, but I promised to keep trying to contact you."

"What does he want?"

"I don't know—he didn't say. All he would tell me is that he needs to talk to you."

"I'll call him," he told her.

"How was the summit?" Angela asked.

"High. And cold. And snowy," Zach said drily. "I notice you didn't ask if I made it to the top."

"Of course not," she said with cool confidence. "I've never known you to fail. We'll have champagne when you get back to the office, boss."

Zach laughed. "You're buying, right?"

"Absolutely. The grocery store carries bubbly."

Zach groaned and his assistant laughed, her amusement clear despite the intermittent static. After she'd assured him there were no other urgent matters at the office, they said goodbye and hung up.

It took a few moments to place the call from the satellite phone in Nepal to Cade's cell phone back in the States.

"Cade, it's Zach."

"Where the hell have you been, Zach?" Cade's deep voice demanded. Once again, the line crackled with interference.

"Climbing Mount Everest in Nepal," Zach told him without missing a beat, amused at his older brother's growl. "We made it to the top and are on our way down. At the moment, I'm in a tent at base camp."

"Good to know you survived," Cade said. "There's no easy way to say this, Zach." His voice was suddenly solemn, grim. "The old man died. He left the Triple C to you, me, Eli and Brodie. I'm in Indian Springs and I need you to come home."

"Hell." Zach was stunned and barely aware he spoke aloud as he tried to get his head around Cade's words. Joseph Coulter was gone—and his sons were his heirs? How was that possible? He shook his head to clear it, focusing on his brother's last sentence. "I always said I'd never go back there, Cade, but if you need me, I'm on my way. Have you talked to Eli and Brodie?"

"I left a message on Eli's machine asking him to call me but I haven't heard from him. And I have no idea where the hell Brodie is. The last phone number I had for him isn't good anymore. Have you heard from him over the last six to eight months?"

Zach frowned, trying to recall. "No, I think it's been more like ten months. Last I remember, he was still on the road following the rodeo circuit. We talked about meeting up in Oregon this summer to go white water rafting and fly-fishing on the Rogue River."

"Damn." Cade's disappointment carried clearly over the line, as if he were standing in the tent with Zach instead of thousands of miles away. "I was hoping you'd talked to him."

"We'll find him, Cade," Zach said. "None of us ever goes a year without checking in. If he and Eli haven't called you before I reach Indian Springs, I'll have Angela start searching, too." His assistant was as reliable as a bloodhound at tracking down information. "I'll head out as soon as I can. First, I have to get off the mountain and there's a storm kicking up so just leaving Nepal might take a while."

"All right. Let me know if you need a ride from the

airport. And Zach…" Cade paused, his voice rougher, deeper when he continued. "I'm glad you're coming home."

"It'll be good to see you, Cade," Zach told him, his voice quiet. "It's been too long. And don't worry about Eli and Brodie—we'll find them."

"Right. See you soon."

And Cade hung up.

Zach switched off the satellite phone and frowned, staring unseeingly at the black plastic. He hadn't seen his father since he and his brothers left the Triple C ranch thirteen years earlier. He hadn't had any contact at all with Joseph Coulter—and he'd been fine with that, relieved even. So why did he feel a wave of sadness at the news that his father was gone?

A swift mental image of Joseph's furious face the morning he'd left was quickly replaced by the same face, warm with affection, before Zach's mother died.

That's why I feel sad, Zach thought. *Because there was a time when life on the Triple C was good.*

But the good times ended for her family when Melanie Coulter died. Joseph became a different man—a man who hated his sons and blamed them for her death.

Zach shoved the painful emotions deep and forced himself to focus. He couldn't do anything to change the past. He had to deal with the present. His mind raced as he considered the logistics necessary to leave the Asian continent and return to Montana.

And the home he'd left behind years ago.

"What's the weather report for tomorrow, Ajax?" he asked, turning to the team leader. "I need to get off the mountain. Now."

Chapter One

Indian Springs, Montana

A week later, Zach stepped out of the Billings, Montana airport terminal at just after 1:00 p.m. and was welcomed by warm spring weather.

Normally he enjoyed the adventure of travel, but for once he was damn glad to have solid ground under his feet. Swinging his loaded duffel bag over his shoulder, he raised a hand to hail a taxi.

He left the lot at Haagensen's Auto Rentals driving a new pickup truck an hour later, the leasing documents tossed on the passenger seat beside him as he headed north toward Indian Springs and the Triple C Ranch, where he'd grown up. He hadn't been in eastern Montana for thirteen years—not since he and his brothers, Cade, Brodie and Eli had left the Triple C the day after Eli, the youngest, graduated from high school. They'd all sworn they'd never come back, and Zach had mixed feelings about returning even now. But Cade had said he needed him and his brother rarely asked for anything.

In fact, Zach thought as he slipped sunglasses on the bridge of his nose, he couldn't remember the last time Cade had asked him for a favor.

He made good time, even making a quick stop for a much-needed cup of coffee. When he was fifty miles south of Indian Springs, his cell phone rang. A quick glance at caller ID made him smile.

"Yo, Cade, what's up?"

"Zach, glad I reached you. Where are you?"

"About fifty miles out. I should be there in less than an hour."

"Can you stop at Ned Anderson's law office in town first?" Cade asked. "He has documents for you and the keys to the Lodge."

"Can I see him tomorrow? I'd rather come straight to the Triple C."

"You could—but it would be better if you talked to Ned first."

"All right. But you owe me, and as soon as I sleep for about forty-eight hours and can function again, I'm collecting."

Cade's deep chuckle sounded over the connection. "Just as long as it's food or a bed, you've got it. Anything else and you might be out of luck."

"Works for me. See you in a couple of hours."

Zach disconnected before he remembered he hadn't asked Cade why he wanted the lodge keys picked up. And why Cade hadn't collected them himself.

Oh, well, he thought with a mental shrug. *I'll see the attorney, then head out to the ranch. Then I'll find a bed and sleep until tomorrow. Or maybe the next day.*

He rubbed his eyes; the inside of his lids felt as if they'd been sifted with sand. He'd lost track of time somewhere during the endless round of waiting for trains and planes, and he couldn't remember how long it had been since he'd slept more than a couple of consecutive hours. Weariness dragged at him.

He rolled his shoulders, picked up his coffee and swallowed the barely drinkable brew. Caffeine had kept him going this far, he reflected. It would have to do for a few hours more.

He reached the outskirts of Indian Springs and within minutes was driving down Main Street in the center of the small town. He scanned the businesses, locating the attorney's sign halfway down a block, and angled his truck into a parking spot.

He yawned, scrubbed a palm over his face and stepped out of the pickup and onto the curb before he stopped abruptly, riveted by the sight of the petite blonde standing a few yards away with her back to him. Tired though he was, testosterone fired off rockets, sending adrenaline racing through his bloodstream and erasing his weariness as if it had never existed.

He was so focused on the gleam of sunlight in silky blond hair and the slim, curved body in snug jeans and red sweater that he paid little attention to the man she was talking to.

But then the pretty blonde moved to walk on and the older man shifted to stop her.

Her shoulders moved in a faint shudder before she lifted her head, her body tense.

Oh, hell, no. A surge of protectiveness had Zach stepping forward as he heard the woman's clear feminine voice ask the man to step aside.

Cynthia Deacon left the small but well-stocked department store on Main Street and stepped out into the warm afternoon sunshine. A shopping bag holding a new pair of crimson lace bikini panties dangled from the fingers of one hand.

Slipping sunglasses onto the bridge of her nose, she strolled down the sidewalk. The weather was warm for a May afternoon in northeast Montana. The old-timers in town were predicting an early summer with temperatures hotter than usual.

Indulging in window shopping was a rare luxury for Cynthia. Until three weeks ago, her daily routine meant long hours on the job managing high-end hotels around the world and most recently, that meant a posh hotel in Palm Springs, California. She'd resigned abruptly, however, when her boss made it clear he expected her duties to include sexual favors.

She had no regrets that she'd stood up for her principles. Being unemployed, however, was shockingly outside her comfort zone. She'd worked nearly nonstop since she was sixteen—part-time during high school and while studying at Harvard, and full-time thereafter. She'd spent the day after resigning sending out résumés and calling or emailing her business connections to let them know she was looking for a new position. Then she'd packed her bags, moved out of her rooms at the

hotel and driven north from Palm Springs to her childhood home in Montana. She'd been putting off dealing
with her great-uncle's estate for several months and her
unexpected free time seemed the perfect opportunity
to do so.

Today, though, she refused to worry about being unemployed. Instead, she embraced the novelty of leisurely
shopping and dawdling along Main Street in the small
ranching community where she'd grown up.

She stopped and pulled off her sunglasses to look
more closely at a window display just as the throaty
growl of a powerful engine broke the sleepy afternoon
quiet. She glanced over her shoulder and saw a black
pickup truck nose into a parking spot behind her. The
vehicle's tinted windows prevented her from seeing the
driver clearly and she turned back to the boots displayed
in the store window.

She'd been considering buying the pair of turquoise-
and-black Tony Lama cowboy boots for the past week.
Being temporarily unemployed, she knew she should
stay on a budget, but the boots were seriously gorgeous.
She could almost hear them whisper her name, calling
to her each time she walked past the window.

A quick burst of loud music startled her and she
glanced sideways down the sidewalk to her left. A beefy,
middle-aged man in jeans and a cowboy hat exited the
open door of Slocums Bar and walked toward her. Behind him, the heavy door swung shut, cutting off the
music and crowd noise.

Cynthia registered the swift interest and smile on the
man's face before she turned back to the window, hoping
he'd take the not-so-subtle hint and walk on by.

"Well, hello there."

Cynthia nearly groaned aloud at the suggestive note in the male voice. She didn't turn around, although experience told her it was unlikely he'd leave her alone.

"Didn't you hear me?" The voice was closer. A hand cupped her shoulder.

With a practiced move, Cynthia slipped from beneath his touch and turned to face him.

"I beg your pardon," she said with cool precision. "You must have mistaken me for someone you actually know."

She didn't recognize the man but the interest gleaming in his brown eyes was all too familiar.

"But I'd like to get to know you. You're the prettiest thing I've seen in a long time." His gaze swept over her, lingering on her breasts. His smile widened, creasing his florid face. "Let me buy you a drink," he said, his voice heavy with innuendo. "We'll get acquainted."

"Sadly," she said, her voice icy enough to chill, "I'm afraid I have to turn you down."

"Aw, come on, honey," he coaxed. "You'll like me if you spend a little time with me."

Cynthia moved to step around him.

He shifted sideways, blocking her.

"Let me pass," she said tightly, ruthlessly holding down a wave of panic. She hated the feeling, hated being unable to control it, especially since she knew on a rational level that it was unlikely the man was a serious threat. Not on Main Street in broad daylight. At the end of the block, two young mothers strolled, three little boys bouncing along beside them down the sidewalk. Despite knowing she wasn't alone on the street with the man, Cynthia couldn't stop the instant shudder that shook her.

"The lady said step aside." A different deep male voice held cold authority.

The man's face tightened into a belligerent scowl as his gaze moved past her. Whatever he saw made his eyes widen, as the ruddy color leached out of his face and he immediately took a step back.

Cynthia drew a deep breath and fought for control. She half turned to look over her shoulder and felt her own eyes widen as she caught her breath at the sight of the man standing a few feet behind her.

He was over six feet tall with broad shoulders and long legs. Beard stubble shadowed his jaw and his coal-black hair looked several weeks overdue for a haircut. The hard angles of his face were set in implacable lines and beneath the slash of dark eyebrows, his grass-green eyes were narrowed and focused on the other man in a menacing stare. He wore a scarred brown leather bomber jacket that hung open over a black T-shirt and faded jeans with scuffed black cowboy boots. The jeans had apparently seen so many washings that they were faded white at stress points, the soft worn denim stretched over the powerful muscles of his thighs.

He looked as if he'd ridden straight in off the range, packing a six-gun and looking for trouble, Cynthia thought with disbelief. There was something vaguely familiar about him but she couldn't quite put her finger on it.

That deep, cold voice prompted the other man. "I think it's time you moved on."

"Uh, yeah." The shorter man touched his hat with a

quick nod at Cynthia and turned on his heel to hurry off down the sidewalk.

"Are you all right?" The stranger turned his gaze on her and Cynthia was transfixed.

Dangerous, she thought. *This gorgeous male could be seriously dangerous.*

"I'm fine," she assured him, gathering her wits. "He was annoying but I don't think he would have actually hurt me."

The stranger smiled, white teeth flashing in his tanned face, turning him from lethal to the poster boy for male charm.

"I certainly hope not," he drawled. "Unless Indian Springs has changed drastically, women don't normally have to worry about being assaulted on Main Street." He cocked his head to the side and eyed her with interest. "It's been a long time since I lived here, but I don't ever remember anyone in town as pretty as you."

Cynthia laughed, amusement bubbling at his obvious line. "I grew up here," she told him. She was immensely relieved to find she was comfortable with his flirting. Lots of men had flirted with her over the years and she usually enjoyed the fencing with words that ensued. It wasn't until someone stepped into her personal space and wouldn't accept a refusal, as the older man had earlier, that she lost her composure and felt threatened.

"Not possible," he promptly denied. "I would have remembered you. I have an infallible memory for beautiful women."

"And I bet you've known a lot of them," she shot back, smiling when he winced and grinned at her.

His eyes twinkled, only slightly easing the heat in his green gaze.

Cynthia hadn't felt this attracted to a man in…well, she realized, never. Though he was clearly a heart-breaker, he was undeniably charming and just as clearly, interested in her.

"I'm Zach Coulter," he said.

Her eyes widened and her breath caught. *Of course you are,* she thought. *I should have realized the moment I saw you.* All the Coulter boys had coal-black hair, green eyes and lady-killer charm. It was part of what made them so unforgettable.

She was five years younger than Zach, and he'd grad-uated from high school while she was still in junior high. Cynthia wasn't surprised that he didn't remember her because she'd simply been too young for him to notice. But she suspected most females who saw the Coulter brothers before they left town hadn't forgotten them—and that included her.

"And you are…?" he prompted with the lift of a brow.

"Cynthia Deacon." She held out her hand and felt it immediately enclosed in hard masculine warmth. His grip was firm, the surface of his palm and fingers faintly rough with calluses.

"Cynthia." He repeated her name slowly, as if savor-ing the sound of it on his lips. Then his mouth curved upward in a small, wholly male smile. "It's nice to meet you."

"Likewise," she told him, tugging gently to free her fingers. "I'm sorry about your father. I'd heard your oldest brother was back at the Triple C, but the local grapevine said he was the only Coulter who'd returned."

"He was until today." Zach nodded briefly in confirmation. "I just got in."

"From where?" Cynthia knew her question was impolite but curiosity overrode good manners.

"Nepal."

She felt her eyes widen again. "Nepal? What on earth were you doing there?"

His eyes laughed at her as his white teeth flashed in a grin. "I was climbing Mount Everest."

"Seriously?" Nonplussed, she stared at him, speechless. "I think you're the first person I've ever met who even attempted that. Did you reach the top?"

"Summit," he corrected her. "And yes, we did."

"What was it like?" She stared at him, wondering what drove a man to climb mountains covered in snow and ice.

"Cold," he told her gravely. "Really cold."

Startled, she laughed out loud. Amusement lit his features and laugh lines crinkled at the corners of his eyes.

"What? You don't believe me?" he asked mildly.

"Oh, I believe you," she said hastily. "I just can't believe that's the first thing that comes to mind when you've climbed a mountain most people only dream of attempting."

He shrugged, broad shoulders shifting beneath the leather jacket.

"It was…awe inspiring." The teasing quality was gone from his voice. "Like standing on top of the world."

If she'd been attracted earlier by his teasing smile

and unconcealed male interest, she found herself even more powerfully drawn by the depth and sincerity in his words.

"It must have been amazing," she said with a sigh. "I've never had an experience like that. The highest I've ever been—outside an airplane—is standing on top of the Empire State Building's observation deck and looking down on the streets of New York."

"I've done that, too." He smiled down at her, easy charm once more in place. "I liked it."

"So did I," she said drily. "But it hardly compares with climbing Mount Everest."

"Maybe, but it's much warmer. And there aren't as many obstacles along the way, which is always a plus," he commented. "As hallmark experiences go, there's a lot to be said for the Empire State Building's observation deck."

She shook her head, smiling. "If we're comparing dangerous experiences, I'm betting climbing scary-high mountain wins."

He chuckled, the sound reverberating and sending shivers up her spine.

No wonder he had a reputation as a heartbreaker back in high school, Cynthia thought, blinking against the sudden urge to step closer, lay her hand on his chest to feel his heartbeat and tuck her face against the warm, strong column of his throat to breathe in the subtle scent of his aftershave. *I need to get a grip.*

Before she could comment, the patter of feet on concrete sounded behind her, accompanied by the shrieks of children.

"Douglas, watch where you're going!" a feminine voice warned.

The cautionary warning came too late. One of the little boys crashed into Cynthia from behind, knocking her forward.

And straight into Zach.

Her hands rested on his chest and his arms instantly wrapped around her. She was swamped with a flood of emotions—desire, and an odd sense of security. He was much taller than she and the top of her head barely reached his chin. The body she pressed against was solid and strong, the muscles of his chest hard where her palms flattened against him. Up close, the curve of his mouth was unbelievably seductive and his green eyes darkened as she stared.

Belatedly realizing she was lying against him, unmoving, she stirred and his arms instantly loosened. His hands shifted to her shoulders, his firm hold steadying her as she stepped back before he released her fully.

"I'm so sorry. Are you all right?" A worried female voice broke the spell.

Cynthia glanced over her shoulder at the flustered young mother, her gaze dropping to the little boy the woman held firmly by the hand.

"Yes." She managed a shaky smile as she turned to face them. "Yes, I'm fine. No harm done."

Relief moved over the young woman's face. "Thank goodness." She bent to the little boy. "Douglas, apologize to the lady."

"Sorry." The child looked up at Cynthia through thick lashes.

He was adorable. Charmed, she couldn't be upset with him.

"That's okay," she said, smiling at him.

He rewarded her with an ear-to-ear grin that lit his face before he bashfully ducked his head.

With a final apology, the two women and their charges set off down the street.

Drawing a deep, steadying breath, Cynthia turned to face Zach.

His green gaze was intent, focused on her. She was instantly swamped with the memory of his arms around her, the sensation of her body pressed against his.

"Thanks for catching me," she said. The effort to appear cool and unaffected by those brief moments took all her control.

"Anytime." His mouth curved in a slow, wholly masculine smile.

Cynthia's heartbeat stuttered before settling in a faster, harder rhythm.

With great effort, she pulled her gaze from his mouth and glanced at her watch. "Well, it was lovely to meet you, Zach—and welcome back to Indian Springs. I have to run. I have an appointment." As she spoke, she took several backward steps down the sidewalk. "I'm sure I'll see you around. It's such a small town." She smiled vaguely and turned on her heel. Walking swiftly and purposefully, she headed toward her car that was parked halfway down the block.

And felt his intense gaze with every step she took.

Zach watched her go, surprised at the speed with which she'd gone from friendly conversation to abrupt departure. His gaze tracked her smooth, graceful walk, the slight sway of her hips and the silky blond ponytail that brushed against her shoulders with each step.

Tired though he was after days of travel and little sleep, every cell in his body had snapped to attention the minute he'd seen her. Riveted, his eyes had swept her from head to toe, his body tightening as he did. Her legs were encased in snug jeans, and the red stiletto heels on her small feet made her legs look even longer. Her hair brushed against the red sweater she wore. A shopping bag and small leather handbag dangled from one hand.

He'd only been a few feet away when she attempted to step around the older, beefy cowboy blocking her path.

Zach registered the instant tenseness that gripped the slim, curvy female body.

Then she'd turned and he'd seen her face. Heart-shaped, with dark brows winging above deep blue eyes, high cheekbones, a stubborn little chin below a lush mouth—she was outrageously feminine.

The swift urge to protect and claim swept through him.

Down the sidewalk, Cynthia stepped off the curb and opened the driver's door of a bright red sports car. A moment later, she backed out of the parking slot and drove away.

Zach shook his head. He hadn't reacted to a woman with this much instant lust since he was a teenager. He shrugged and turned to stride to the entrance of the Anderson Law Office only yards away.

It must be the lack of sleep, he told himself.

Even as he blamed his reaction to Cynthia on exhaustion, Zach knew he was lying. He had to admit she'd knocked him off stride without trying, and when she'd smiled…

Damn, he thought ruefully. Just thinking about her smiling up at him was enough to make him want to turn around, find her and see if he could tease her into laughing again.

He realized he was standing outside the law office door, a half smile on his face, and shook his head to clear it.

He needed to focus on seeing the attorney and heading out to the Triple C.

He couldn't help but wonder what Ned Anderson might reveal about his father—and if the attorney could explain why Joseph Coulter had named his sons in his will. Zach had avoided any thoughts about his estranged father for so long that having to talk about him felt strange—and oddly painful.

He steeled himself and pushed open the door.

Chapter Two

Chimes rang, announcing his presence as Zach entered the attorney's office.

"Is Ned Anderson in?" he asked the receptionist.

"No, I'm sorry, he's not. Do you have an appointment?" The older woman eyed him over half-glasses.

"No. My brother told me to stop and talk to him before I head home, but if he's not available I'll come back tomorrow." Zach turned toward the door, not the slightest disappointed that the lawyer wasn't in. He'd rather be at the ranch, sleeping in a warm bed, instead of meeting with his father's estate attorney. He'd been traveling nonstop for nearly a week to get this far. The journey from the base camp at Mount Everest, where he'd spoken with Cade, had required hiking with stubborn pack mules, a train to the nearest city, and finally several airline flights just to reach the U.S. This morning he'd boarded an 11:00 a.m. flight from Seattle to

Billings, where he'd rented the truck and driven to Indian Springs.

"Wait!" The woman's voice stopped him and he looked back at her. "Are you Zach Coulter?"

"Yeah." He paused to look back at her.

"Mr. Anderson had an emergency in Great Falls today, but he asked me to give you something if you arrived while he was gone." She quickly bustled across the waiting area and entered an office. A second later, she popped back out. "Here it is." She held out a sealed manila envelope and a silver ring holding a collection of metal keys. "He said to tell you the letter and enclosures explain everything and that he'll be back in the office next week. He hopes you'll come in to see him then."

Zach took the keys and envelope from her outstretched hand.

"I'll do that." He nodded and left the office. He returned to his truck, tossing the envelope on the passenger seat and shoving the key ring into his jeans pocket before backing out. As he drove off, he glanced at the wide plate-glass window of the attorney's office. Anderson's receptionist watched him, lifting a hand in a wave of farewell.

He returned the gesture, realizing that he'd forgotten how friendly the people in his hometown could be. He liked the energy and convenience of living in San Francisco. It was the perfect base for someone who traveled as much as he did. But he couldn't remember the last time a business acquaintance in the city had waved goodbye to him.

Zach obeyed the twenty-five miles per hour speed limit, giving him time to assess the buildings and shops lining Main Street. Surprisingly, not much had changed in the thirteen years he'd been gone. The Black Bear Bar and Restaurant still took up the corner across from the pharmacy. The big door of Miller's Feed Store was rolled up and stood open for business. The neon sign over the Indian Springs Café still flashed bright red, and Connors Auto Parts had dusty ranch trucks parked at the curb out front.

There were several small shops he didn't remember but all in all, Zach was pleasantly surprised to find his hometown apparently alive and well.

Driving through the center of the town where he'd grown up brought a wash of memories. Picking up speed as he drove toward the Triple C, every mile that brought him closer to his boyhood home held even more.

At last he slowed, braked to turn off the highway and drove beneath a tall, welded metal arch that spelled out Coulter Cattle Company in graceful curves. The lane was edged with pastures dotted with sagebrush before it rounded the base of a butte and topped a rise.

Zach braked, letting the engine idle. At nearly five o'clock the late-afternoon sun highlighted the familiar buildings clustered at the foot of a flat-topped butte on the far side of the valley. From this distance, the ranch looked exactly the same as it had on the morning he'd driven away years ago—for what he'd sworn was the last time.

And damned if he wasn't glad to be here, he thought with surprise. He hadn't seen Cade in nearly a year and it was always good to catch up with his brother. As for returning to the ranch? There was an odd mix of reluctance to see the place and an uncomfortable weight on his chest that reminded him of the way he'd felt after his mother had died. That same heaviness had returned when he'd left the Triple C, and again when Cade had told him Joseph was dead.

He shook his head. He'd never spent a lot of time examining his feelings and he didn't plan to start now. It was enough that he wasn't turning the truck around and heading back to San Francisco.

What the hell, he thought with a shrug. Life was full of surprises. He'd never expected to be driving down this road again.

He shifted the truck into gear and left the crest of the hill, following the gravel road as it descended to the valley floor. The wood-and-iron bridge rattled beneath the wheels as he crossed the creek before the road climbed again to reach the buildings.

Zach automatically swung the truck in a wide circle before parking in front of the house with the nose of the truck pointing toward the exit.

An older pickup sat in front of the bunkhouse across the graveled ranch yard, and a newer model silver truck was parked just beyond Zach's pickup.

Guessing the newer vehicle belonged to Cade, Zach grabbed his duffel bag from the jump seat and stepped out, stretching in an attempt to relieve the aches from the long days of nonstop travel.

The gate in the fence to the house yard opened without a creak when he lifted the latch.

Cade had obviously been doing a lot of work on the place, Zach thought as he closed the gate behind him, his gaze assessing the semicircle of buildings facing the house around the large yard. The bunkhouse was freshly painted and although the barn, machine shop and other buildings were weatherworn, the structures appeared to be solid.

He turned back to the house, running a quick glance over the roofline and corners. Fresh white paint and green trim around the windows and doors had the old house looking better than Zach remembered it.

He strode up the walk, crossed the porch and stepped inside without knocking. The aroma of simmering pot roast filled the air and he caught the murmur of a radio from the direction of the kitchen.

"Hello? Anyone home?" He dropped his duffel bag just inside the door. "Cade?"

"We're in the kitchen—come on back," a feminine voice called.

Zach wondered if Cade had hired a housekeeper. He walked down the hall and entered the kitchen just as the woman standing at the stove turned to look over her shoulder. Her eyes widened in surprise before her lips curved in a smile, lighting up her face.

"Hey," he drawled, stopping just inside the door to glance around the room. "I'm looking for Cade—"

The door to the back porch opened and his brother stepped inside, halting abruptly.

"Zach." Cade crossed the room and grabbed him in a brief, hard hug before stepping back. Eyes as green as Zach's narrowed as he stared. "It's good to see you—but damn, you look like hell."

Zach laughed. "And hello to you, too."

Cade laughed and clapped him on the shoulder. "I'm glad you're back. Even if you do look like you haven't slept in a week."

"I probably haven't," Zach drawled. "I plan to say hello and find the nearest empty bed to sleep for a day or two. Have you heard from Eli or Brodie?"

"Not yet. I'm hoping you'll ask your ace assistant to join the search."

Zach shrugged. "Angela's never failed to find whatever she's looked for. Want me to call her?"

"Yeah," Cade said. "Any help she can give us would be great. It can wait until you get some rest, though."

"All right." A movement behind Cade caught Zach's attention and he looked over his brother's shoulder. The pretty blonde was smoothing her fingertips over her lashes, her brown eyes damp.

Cade turned, his gaze following Zach's.

"Mariah, honey." His deep voice gentled and it held a note Zach had never heard from his big brother.

Intrigued, he studied their faces as Cade walked to the woman and slung an arm around her shoulders to pull her close against his side.

"This is Mariah Jones, Zach," Cade said, his quiet voice filled with pride and love. "As soon as I can convince her to settle on a date, we're getting married."

Zach felt his eyes widen, and his gaze sharpened on the woman's beautiful face. She smiled at him before tipping her head back to look up at Cade, the love in her expression matching his brother's.

"I'll be damned," Zach murmured. "Congratulations, Cade. And welcome to the family, Mariah." He shook his head, stunned and trying to absorb the fact that his oldest brother was in love. "Never thought I'd see the day when one of us got married."

Mariah laughed, her smile impish. "You're second born, Zach, which means you're next."

"No." He held up his hands, palms out, before crossing his index fingers in the classic gesture to ward off evil. "No way. Not gonna happen."

Cade's deep chuckle blended with Mariah's laughter.

A sudden yawn caught Zach by surprise and he scrubbed his hand down his face, feeling the scratch of beard stubble. "Sorry," he apologized. Exhaustion hit him like a wave. "I haven't slept much over the last few days. Not to mention the time zone change. I'm jet-lagged *and* sleep-deprived."

"We weren't sure how long it would take you to get here, but as soon as you called from Nepal we put clean sheets and blankets on the bed in your old room," Cade said. "Why don't you head upstairs? We can talk later."

"Sounds like a plan," Zach agreed. "Nice to meet you, Mariah. Will I see you later?"

"I'll be around when you wake up," she told him.

"Good." He nodded and turned away. "Good night, you two." He lifted a hand in farewell, their echoes of "good night" following him down the hall. He paused at the front door to collect his duffel bag and then climbed the stairs to the second floor. The door to his old bedroom stood open and he turned on the bedside lamp, dropping his duffel on the bed before closing the door.

He was too tired to do more than give the room a cursory inspection but did register that while the furniture was the same, someone had hung new curtains. The room was clean, the top of the pine wood dresser where he dropped his wallet and assorted clutter from his pockets dust-free.

He shucked off his boots and jeans, pulled his shirt off over his head and clad in only his boxers, slid between the sheets.

Just before he fell asleep, he thought about how Cynthia Deacon had fit into his arms as if custom made just for him. And he wondered how long it would be before he could see her again.

Chapter Three

Cynthia couldn't stop thinking about Zach Coulter. She'd felt his gaze burning into her as she'd walked to her car, and hadn't been able to resist checking him out in her rearview mirror as she drove away. He'd stood on the sidewalk without moving, staring after her.

He wasn't shy about letting a woman know he found her attractive, she thought, her lips tilting upward at the corners as she remembered the interest in his green eyes while they'd talked. She'd met a lot of good-looking men at the hotels where she'd worked over the past few years and more than a few had made passes at her. But Zach raised "handsome and charming" to a whole new level.

At dinnertime she pulled open the refrigerator door in her kitchen and took out red leaf lettuce, a slim English cucumber, tomato, avocado and a red bell pepper. Standing at the counter, she rinsed and, with practiced, efficient movements, quickly chopped, sliced and diced.

She wondered how long he would be in town.

She paused, knife in hand, and looked out the window above the sink at the backyard, lit by late afternoon sun. The big elm tree in the far corner was in full leaf, the spreading branches shading the white picket fence and at least six feet of elderly Mrs. Riley's yard next door. The snowball bush along the back fence was covered in fist-sized clusters of green buds that would pop into circles of white flowers.

Neatly edged in brick, the flower beds along the one-car garage in the corner opposite the elm tree were raked, fertilized and seeded.

The old house and the gardens her great-uncle Nicholas had loved were ready for summer. She vividly remembered working beside him, her small hands next to his gnarled fingers as they tucked the roots of green living plants into warm black soil. The gentle elderly man, his garden and home had been a haven of peace and sanity in a childhood threatened by her mother's chaotic lifestyle.

How long will I be in town, Cynthia wondered. She'd sent out résumés immediately after her arrival, but she'd been back in Indian Springs and the welcoming old house for almost two weeks. She'd readied the flower beds and seeded them, aired out the upstairs bedrooms and folded away winter bedding, trimmed and fertilized the roses along the front porch. She'd certainly been busy. But she hadn't received any response to her résumés, nor to any applications online.

Cynthia opened a cupboard door and took out a rose-colored Depression-era glass salad bowl and a matching stemmed glass. Long before she and her mother had come to live at his house, Nicholas had lost his beloved wife, Min. He'd continued to care for her lovely glass, crystal, silver and the house's antique furnishings as if doing so had somehow kept a part of her with him. He'd taught Cynthia a deep appreciation for fine old things and given her one of her great-aunt Min's handmade quilts when she'd left Indian Springs to go to college. The quilt had traveled with her ever since and was currently spread out over the foot of her bed upstairs.

As she filled the bowl with tossed salad, layered chilled shrimp atop and drizzled balsamic vinegar and oil over all, she considered what to do with Nicholas's cherished home and furnishings.

The question had plagued her over the weeks since Nicholas had passed away. He'd been ninety-two and although his body had become frail, he'd always been spry and fit with a sharp mind. On some level, she knew she'd simply refused to think about him ever being gone. But now, he was. *And here I am,* she thought as she carried her salad, glass of water and silverware into the adjoining dining room.

Her work required her to travel and she'd always loved that aspect. But it also prevented her from settling in any one spot, limiting her ability to create the kind of home with treasured furnishings that Nicholas had entrusted to her.

She glanced around the room with its long, graceful table and tall sideboard. The table had room to easily accommodate eight people and she knew there were additional leaves and chairs that allowed the table to expand and seat twelve.

Nicholas should have left his home to someone with a big family, she thought as she sipped her water and ate her salad. *I'll never fill these chairs with a husband and children.*

Not that she didn't want to marry and have children. She'd always dreamed that someday she'd find the right man and fall in love. But given her trust issues, she wasn't sure that was possible.

Cynthia sighed, frowning. She'd never been particularly fond of any of her mother's boyfriends, but it wasn't until she was twelve years old that she'd learned to fear men. That was the year the man who'd been dating her mother had caught her alone in the house. By the time Nicholas arrived and pulled the man off of her, she'd been bruised and terrified, her lip cut and her blouse torn. Her mother had been furious—at her, not the boyfriend. And despite counseling during college, Cynthia had never been able to move past the suffocating panic when a male acted aggressively.

Which is why I'll probably never marry, she thought, staring at the empty chairs ranged along the sides and the far ends of the table.

She had an unexpected, instant mental image of Zach Coulter, eyes alight with amusement as he smiled at her, sitting at the head of the table on her left.

"Not likely," she said aloud in the silent room. She shook her head, popping a pink shrimp into her mouth. "He's out of my league. If I ever consider looking for a husband, I should probably start with a basic small-sedan-level guy. Zach's more like a high-performance-sports-car-level guy. Still," she mused with a sigh, "a girl can dream."

Her voice seemed loud in the hushed room.

"I'm talking to myself," she muttered. "Definitely time to find a new job with real people to talk to."

She rose and walked back into the kitchen to switch on the radio on the shelf just inside the door. When she returned to the table, the muted strains of Memphis blues followed her, filling the hushed, waiting silence.

Determinedly, she turned her attention to finishing her dinner and her thoughts to job hunting and considering whether to tweak her résumé.

But when she turned off the light and settled into her bed later that evening, her last drowsy thought was of Zach's green eyes smiling down at her.

Zach didn't wake until six o'clock the next morning.

By the time he'd showered, shaved and dressed to head downstairs, his stomach was growling. The aroma of coffee teased his nostrils and he followed it down the hallway.

"Morning." He nodded at Cade and Mariah, seated at the heavy wooden table in the far corner of the kitchen. He automatically pulled open the cabinet door above the coffeemaker and took out a mug, only realizing as he filled the cup that he'd remembered where they were kept.

It had been thirteen years since he'd taken a mug from that cupboard, but somewhere buried deep, the memory had lain dormant till needed.

The human mind was a weird and wonderful thing,

he thought, carrying his steaming mug with him to the table.

Just as he pulled out a chair and sat, his stomach growled again, this time more loudly.

"How long since you ate?" Cade asked, his long legs stretched out beneath the table.

"Yesterday," Zach said, sipping his coffee.

"I mean something besides fast food at the airport," Cade said drily.

"Ah." Zach nodded, pursing his lips as he considered. "I think that might have been at a sushi bar in Tokyo."

Mariah's eyes rounded. "How long ago was that?"

"You know," Zach confessed, "I'm not sure. What day is this?"

Cade laughed and Mariah pushed back her chair to stand.

"I'm making you breakfast," she announced, crossing the room to pull open the refrigerator door. "How do you feel about steak, eggs, hash browns and toast?"

"I think I've died and gone to heaven," he told her. "But you don't have to cook for me. I can do it."

She laughed. "We take turns cooking around here so you'll have your chance. For now, sit, talk to Cade and drink your coffee."

"Thanks." Zach looked at Cade. "I think we should keep her."

"*I'm* keeping her," Cade told him with a grin. "You'll have to get your own girl."

Zach had a swift mental image of Cynthia Deacon's face. "I'll see what I can do," he said aloud, deciding Cade's words had only made him think of the pretty blonde because he'd seen her just yesterday. "I stopped at Anderson's office in town. He wasn't there, but his secretary gave me a thick envelope and a set of keys. I haven't opened the envelope yet, but I'm assuming it's a copy of the will."

"Probably," Cade said. "And the keys must be for the Lodge."

"Why am I getting keys to the Lodge?" Zach lifted his cup and sipped, his gaze fastened on his brother's face, which had gone from relaxed to somber.

"Because Dad left the Triple C to all of us in equal shares, but he also left an asset to each of us individually," Cade said. "The Coulter Lodge belongs to you now. You can do anything you want with it."

Zach stared at him. "Why did the old man leave me anything?" he said at last. "He hated my guts."

Cade sighed and scrubbed his hand down his face. "Yeah, that's pretty much how I felt when I heard he'd left us the Triple C." He glanced over his shoulder. "Mariah convinced me the old man had a change of heart. She worked for him and lived here on the ranch for the last several years, took care of him when he got sick. She says he regretted the drinking and everything that came with it. And Wayne says he stopped drinking and became a hermit after we all left."

"He stopped drinking?" Zach stared at Cade. "That's hard to believe." Although if Wayne Smalley had told Cade that Joseph Coulter had given up alcohol, it was hard to dispute the claim. Zach had known his parents' friend, and Wayne's buddies—Asa Kelly and Ben Holcomb, since he was a child.

"I know." Cade nodded in agreement. "But it seems to be true."

Zach lifted his mug and realized he'd emptied it. He pushed back his chair and stood, crossing to the counter and the coffeemaker. Beside him, Mariah removed bread from the toaster and proceeded to spread butter on the slices.

"It's true." She glanced sideways at him, her brown gaze level. "I never saw him take a drink in the three-plus years I've lived here."

"Hmm," Zach responded noncommittally. He'd worked with men who drank too much and concealed it from most people. Where there was a will, there seemed to always be a way. Nonetheless, Mariah apparently was convinced Joseph Coulter had quit the bottle and if she wanted to believe, who was he to question her conviction?

"Tell me about the will," he said as he returned to the table and Cade. "I'll read the entire document and whatever else Anderson put in the envelope later but for now, give me the *Reader's Digest* version."

"It's pretty straightforward," Cade told him. "Dad left everything he had to the four of us—you, me, Eli and Brodie—except for the cabin and the three acres it sits on. He left that to Mariah."

Surprised, Zach's gaze flicked across the room just as Mariah turned from the stove with a steaming plate of food. She met his gaze calmly as she slid the plate of steak, eggs, hash browns and toast on the tabletop in front of him.

"Thanks," he murmured. "Looks great."

"You're welcome." She smiled and went back to the counter, returning with a carafe of coffee and setting it in the center of the table before slipping back into her chair.

Zach wasn't sure how he felt about his grandparents cabin being given away outside the family, but Cade seemed fine with it. He decided to question his brother later, outside Mariah's hearing.

"Go on." He nudged Cade as he cut into the steak and began to eat.

"As I told you earlier, Dad left each of us individual assets that we solely control. He left me the livestock except for the horses, Eli gets Mom's studio and the contents and Brodie has the horses. And you got the Lodge."

Zach lifted his head, his attention caught. "What horses? Are the Kigers still here?"

Cade shrugged. "I don't know—haven't gone looking for them. Figured I'd leave that for Brodie to find out."

"Hard to believe Dad didn't sell the Kigers," Zach commented. "Mom loved those mustangs and he got rid of everything she loved when she died."

"That's what I thought," Cade agreed. "But since I've been back, I learned he did several things that didn't make sense. For instance, he left longhorns in the far pasture. They interbred with Brahma stock and Herefords that probably escaped the lower pastures and climbed into the rough country. We rounded up enough rodeo stock and whitefaces to make a payment on the taxes."

"Why didn't Dad sell them years ago?" Zach asked, puzzled. "It wasn't like him to let an asset sit idle, especially not cattle."

Cade glanced at Mariah, then back at Zach. "Mariah says he was sick for several years before he died. It's possible he didn't have the energy to drive them in and brand them."

"Hmm." Zach considered Cade's words. It was hard to picture his father without the physical strength and energy to run the Triple C. The last time he'd seen Joseph, he was a strong, physically powerful man. He shook off the questions that rose with the thought and looked at his brother. "So tell me the bad news. None of this sounds like you'd need my input. What's wrong?"

"The inheritance taxes are astronomical and there are no cash assets."

Zach went still, eyes narrowing over Cade. "So we have to sell?" he asked slowly, surprised at the instant rejection of the idea that slammed into him.

"That's one option," Cade agreed. "But it's one we can't take without all four of us agreeing. And, so far, you and I are the only ones here."

"You mean we all have to agree before we can sell any sections of land?" Zach guessed shrewdly.

"Exactly." Cade nodded and leaned forward, his forearms resting on the table, his mug cupped between his hands. "As I said, I rounded up cattle and sold off all I could to make a payment on the taxes. Anderson said it bought us some time, but we're going to need a hell of a lot more to clear the tax debt."

"No other assets?" Zach asked. "What about Mom's collections—and Dad's. Did he sell them all off after we left?" Zach had vivid memories of the art, antiques and historical artifacts his parents had gathered. His favorite had been the dozens of wagons, buggies and other conveyances that had filled a huge storage building a mile from the ranch house.

"If any of Mom's sculptures were in her studio when Dad locked the doors and sealed the building after she died, they have the potential to be very valuable. Mom's more famous now than she was when she was alive and working. And if Brodie decides to sell some of the horses—if there are any horses—they could be worth quite a bit." Cade paused to lift his mug and drink. "And if you find a way to raise money with the Lodge, it could go a long way to paying off the tax debt. I'm assuming you don't have a few extra million sitting in a bank account that you'd be willing to use?" he added drily, his lips quirking.

"Me?" Zach shook his head. "I have investments, but nothing I can liquidate to get that kind of cash." He eyed Cade. "Exactly how much money are we talking about here, in round figures?"

The amount Cade quoted had Zach whistling softly.

"That's a hell of a lot of zeroes," he said. "If we all agreed, what about selling off some acres of land to raise the money?"

"We could do that," Cade told him. "But if we do, the size of the Triple C would be radically reduced. And if we want to keep it, we'd have a hard time making it profitable."

"So we either find a way between the four of us to raise the money to pay the taxes, or we sell the ranch intact, pay off the taxes, split what's left between the four of us and walk away."

"That's about the size of it," Cade agreed.

"Hell." Zach pushed his empty plate away and leaned back in his chair, frowning at his brother. "I vote to keep the place. But I don't like the odds of our being able to raise that kind of money."

"And we can't have a definitive plan until we talk to Eli and Brodie," Cade finished for him.

"Exactly." Zach crossed his arms over his chest and narrowed his eyes over his brother's face, considering. "But I'd bet my life neither of them will want to sell." He looked at Mariah, then back at Cade. "It's unlikely I'll stay in Montana when all this is over. But you two—" he gestured at them "—you're going to live here and work the ranch, right?"

Cade's gaze met Mariah's and she smiled faintly, nodding at him.

"Yeah," he said with surety. "We'd like to raise our kids here."

"Kids." Zach was suddenly sidetracked by the memory of himself and his three brothers swimming in the creek on a hot summer day, riding horses at breakneck speed over the prairie, or climbing the butte behind the house to get closer to the stars hanging in the velvety black night sky. Yeah, he thought, this would be a good place for kids if Cade was their father. "You plan to make me an uncle?"

"Sure." Cade grinned him, deep green eyes lit with amusement.

"Damn." Zach shook his head in mock disbelief. He couldn't remember seeing Cade this happy in years. He winked at Mariah. "Are you sure you want to take him on? He was hell on wheels as a kid—what if you have a boy like him?"

"I'd love it," she answered promptly.

The sound of an engine turning over sounded from outside and Cade glanced at his watch.

"That must be Pete taking J.T. to the bus stop," he said. "It's later than I thought."

"A bus stop? Have we got school kids living here?"

"Just one," Cade told him. "J.T. Butler is in high school. He works before and after school, on weekends and vacations, and lives in the bunkhouse with an older ranch hand, Pete Smith."

"How many other employees?" Zach asked.

"None."

Zach eyed Cade. "You're kidding, right?"

"Nope, that's it."

"So the three of you are running the Triple C?"

"Pretty much." Cade's grin told Zach he understood his disbelief.

"Hell." Zach shook his head and muttered, "The hits just keep on comin'."

"Yeah. The good news is the Turner brothers still own their place and they've been helping out. A lot," Cade told him. "And the neighbors all pitched in to help when we rounded up the cattle."

"Thank God for that." Zach couldn't believe two men and Mariah had been working the Triple C. The ranch needed a crew big enough to fill the bunkhouse. Even when his father, Zach and his three brothers were all working, they'd still had several hired hands. Clearly, life on the Triple C had changed drastically over the years. And if he was going to contribute to paying off the tax debt, he'd better take a look at the condition of the ranch and the Lodge to get a better idea of just what he and his brothers were facing. "What are you doing today?" Zach asked Cade.

"Nothing that can't be put off until tomorrow if you want company."

Zach stretched, shoving one hand into the pocket of his faded jeans to pull out the small metal ring with its set of keys. He contemplated it for a moment, then looked at Cade. "Let's open up the Lodge."

Cade nodded. "Sounds like a plan."

Zach shoved back his chair and stood, carrying his dirty dishes to the sink where he rinsed them off and slotted them into the dishwasher rack.

"I'll grab my hat and be down in a minute," he said. As he left the room, he caught a quick glimpse of Cade bending to brush a kiss against Mariah's mouth.

He wondered how she'd managed to get close enough to Cade to get under his skin, let alone capture his heart. Cade had always sworn he would never fall in love and marry. He'd claimed he carried too much baggage after enduring their father's misery and alcoholism following their mother's death.

Hell, he thought. *We probably all do.* It was good to see Cade had found a woman he wanted to share his life with.

Mariah was wrong if she thought Zach would ever get married, though. He loved women, but marriage? Not in the cards. His lifestyle had him traveling often for work and his love of adventure did the same, which left little time or space to consider settling down. It wouldn't be fair to ask a woman to put up with his absence from home two-thirds of the year.

But in a flash of stark honesty, Zach realized that was

the stock answer he'd been giving for years to anyone who quizzed him about his bachelor status.

It was all true, but it wasn't the whole story.

If he were being honest, he knew he had the same reasons for avoiding marriage that Cade had. His parents had seemed happy and deeply in love before his mother died. After her death, Joseph had plunged into an abyss of grief and alcoholism, dragging his sons with him into their own particular hell.

Zach couldn't remember exactly when he'd made the decision, but within a few years of his mother's death, he'd vowed to never love anyone as much as his father had loved his mother.

And if Cade had leftover baggage from their childhood spent struggling to deal with Joseph's alcoholic rages and violence, then Zach was sure he did, too, despite the years he'd spent in counseling.

Still, he wondered if there was a possibility that someday, a woman might look at him like Mariah looks at Cade.

The swift image of Cynthia's soft mouth curving in a smile as she looked up at him, blue eyes warm with amusement, made his step falter.

He barely knew her, had only spent a few moments talking with her. Yet he couldn't help but wonder what it would be like to have her look at him with love.

Chapter Four

When Zach came back downstairs, Cade was waiting at the front door and they left the house together.

Zach paused on the porch, sweeping an assessing glance over the property. His ability to analyze and predict the potential of businesses had brought him executive-level success in San Francisco. He reported directly to the CEO of a capital venture firm; it was his responsibility to descend on companies in trouble, analyze their strengths and weaknesses, then recommend either a plan to save them or to dismantle them.

He'd never imagined that expertise would be used on his childhood home.

Though all but the house and bunkhouse were weathered and needed paint, each appeared to be in relatively good condition. What he could see of the fences in the pasture, they were straight and strong, with white-faced Hereford cattle grazing within the barbed wire enclosures.

"I see you've started painting," he commented as he and Cade left the porch and walked to his truck. "Any major repair work needed on the buildings?"

Cade detoured to his own truck, collected a tool-box from the back and returned to set it in the bed of Zach's truck. Then he pulled open the passenger door. "Everything is pretty sound. I haven't had to make any emergency repairs."

Zach halted, hand on the driver's door handle, as a green truck pulled into the yard and stopped on the far side of Cade's vehicle. Zach instantly recognized the driver.

"Hey, Grady." Warm pleasure filled Zach's voice as he greeted his old friend. The six Turner brothers lived on a neighboring ranch, and although Zach was five years older than Grady, they'd been best friends before he left Indian Springs. He purposely hadn't kept in touch with anyone in Montana, but he'd missed Grady and his brothers. "It's good to see you."

"When did you get back?" Grady Turner jumped out of the pickup and jogged across the graveled yard to join him, the two men shook hands and exchanged a brief, hard hug. Grady nodded at Cade before turning back to Zach.

"Just yesterday," Zach replied.

"I heard you were climbing Mt. Everest. How was it?"

"Cold." Zach laughed at the expression on Grady's face.

"How was the trip home?"

"Long."

"Damn." Grady laughed. "I heard Cade reached you overseas."

Zach nodded. "There was a message waiting for me when I descended to base camp."

"Did you make it to the top of the mountain?" Grady asked with interest.

"Hell, yes."

"Should have known." Grady clapped him on the back. "Congratulations."

"How are your brothers?"

"Fine—all five of them. We've all spent some time here on the Triple C over the last few months," Grady said.

"Yeah, Cade told me how great you and your brothers have been." Zach studied his old friend. "I appreciate it. I know Brodie and Eli would tell you the same if they were here."

"Have you heard from your younger brothers?" Grady asked.

"No." Zach shook his head. "I have an assistant who's talented at tracking people and I've asked her to start looking. With luck, she'll find them."

"It's good to see you Coulters here on the Triple C again—since Cade's been back, the place is looking up. And now that you're here, too, things can only get better, right?"

"I sure as hell hope so," Zach said. "We're headed to the old Lodge to take a look inside—want to come with us?"

Grady shook his head. "I'm supposed to meet Mason in town and I'm late already. I just wanted to stop by and say welcome home." Grady held out his hand and Zach took it, the warm firm clasp an affirmation of friendship. "I'm damned glad you're home, Zach." Grady clapped him on the shoulder once again. "You should join me and Mason at the Black Bear on Saturday. The management booked a good local band and you're sure to see people you know. My brothers will probably show up if they're in town."

"I'll be there unless something comes up," Zach promised.

The two men parted; Grady returned to his truck while Zach joined Cade in his pickup.

"Are you ready for this?" Cade asked, his deep voice quiet.

"Ready as I'll ever be," Zach replied, knowing he'd have to steel himself to step into the Lodge. Memories of his mother were sure to blindside him on occasion, especially now that he was back on the ranch she'd loved.

He wondered how she would have felt about the son who caused her death owning the Lodge she'd created.

"I haven't gone inside, but the outside of the Lodge and Mom's studio seem just as solid as the rest of the buildings," Cade said. "Hopefully the interior is fine."

Zach twisted the key in the ignition and shifted the pickup into gear. "We'll soon find out."

They left the ranch yard, following the gravel road past the big barn. Just beyond Mariah's cabin the road curved to follow the creek to the Lodge, a half mile away.

Joseph Coulter had built the Lodge based on his wife's love of the steep-peaked, log skiing lodges where they often vacationed in the mountains near Yellowstone Park. The Coulter Lodge's two-story structure was built of heavy, massive logs, but the deep slant of the metal roof—its once dark red faded now to rose—combined with lots of window glass, always managed to give the solid, substantial building a graceful air. The porches that edged the front and three sides beneath the shelter of the roof's overhang were still welcoming despite the boards nailed over the big windows and doors, sealing them shut.

Zach parked, and he and Cade left the truck, climbing the shallow, wide steps to the porch and the front door.

"These boards look new," Zach commented as he and Cade used hammers and crowbars to pry them loose.

"J.T. and I replaced them not too long ago," Cade told him as Zach ripped the last board free and laid it atop a stack behind them. "Somebody attempted to break in, probably kids."

"Huh." Zach pulled the key ring from his pocket. Much to his surprise, the key slid easily into the lock and after a moment of careful jiggling, turned with a grating squeal. He pushed the door inward and stepped inside, halting abruptly just over the threshold.

Cade joined him, his low whistle echoing in the big lobby.

Sunlight slanted through the open door behind them, throwing a bar of gold across the dust-covered floor. The rest of the lobby was swathed in gloom. Zach could just make out the wagon-wheel chandeliers suspended from the high ceiling at each end of the long room. They appeared to be draped in cobwebs, and what he remembered as iron sconces set at intervals along the walls were only gray shapes beneath more spiderwebs.

The room was eerily silent, the air heavy and still with a musty scent. Zach wondered if this was what archeologists felt when they opened a long-sealed tomb.

He flipped the light switch next to the door frame but as he expected, the power was off.

"Let's get the boards off the windows," he told Cade. "We need more light."

The two headed back outside, leaving the door open, and worked their way around the porch, prying off the two-by-fours and plywood covering the big windows, stacking the lumber in piles as they went.

When at last they finished and returned to enter the lobby, sunlight flooded the big room.

The last time Zach had been here, the lobby had been alive with light, bustling with a throng of partygoers attending a celebration for his parents' wedding anniversary. Now, the burgundy leather sofas and chairs, the gleam of polished wooden floors with deep red and cream wool carpets and the subtle sheen of wax on log walls—all were dulled beneath layers of dust.

As he and Cade walked farther into the lobby, he noticed the undeniable leavings of mice.

"Looks like something bigger than mice have been in here," Cade commented, pointing at protruding stuffing visible at the corners of sofa cushions and littering the floor beneath.

"I hope it's not rats," Zach told him. "I hate rats."

"Might have been raccoons. They can do a lot of damage."

Zach nudged the shredded corner of the dirt-dulled oriental carpet. "Whatever it was, they were destructive."

Cade nodded and walked toward the fireplace at the end of the room. Zach followed, assessing the damage along the way.

"Looks like the fireplace is still standing," Cade commented.

"Yeah. Who knows if it's still functional." Zach bent to lean into the shoulder-high hearth and peer up the chimney. "I guess we won't know until we get up on the roof and check it." He turned, hands on hips, his gaze following the wall to the reception desk. "I'll be damned," he said, stunned. "Mom's mustang sculpture is still here."

Cade followed as Zach strode back down the long room to halt in front of the curved wooden oak counter that served guests at registration. On the wall behind, beneath a layer of dirt, tarnish and cobwebs, hung a four-foot-tall, six-foot-wide sculpture. Melanie Coulter had used her favorite Kiger mare as a model for the lead of four horses in full gallop. Even with the bright metals dark with dirt and tarnish, the mustangs seemed to dominate the wall, threatening to leap down and thunder across the lobby floor to freedom.

"I always thought this was one of the best things Mom ever did," Cade said quietly.

Zach nodded silently. He remembered the days after his mother's funeral, when his father had ridden out early one morning, leading his mother's mare. Joseph Coulter had returned hours later without the mustang.

Zach had always assumed his father had shot the horse, but his father refused to explain.

He knew his father blamed him for his mother's death.

Hell, he thought, he blamed himself for her death. All four boys had been playing in the creek, using a thick rope tied to an overhanging tree limb to swing out over the water. Zach remembered well how he'd teased his mother, daring her to join them.

He'd never forgotten the terror he'd felt when the rope snapped, nor the awful, sickening sound of her head as it hit the nearly submerged rock at the water's edge.

Even now, the sound was clear in his head, and his chest felt caught in a vise.

Zach shook off the memory of that day, forcing himself to concentrate on the present. He'd been eleven years old when his mother died. As he turned in a slow circle, inspecting the interior of the Lodge, he realized it had been at least twenty-two years since anyone had set foot inside the lobby.

"It looks like hell." He shook his head and glanced at Cade. "But given how long it's been closed, we're probably lucky it's only this bad."

Cade nodded slowly, his gaze sweeping the ceiling. "Yeah, I admit I'm surprised it doesn't seem worse." He pointed at a stain on the ceiling in the back corner. "Maybe we spoke too soon. Looks like there might be some water damage."

Zach frowned. "That's not good." He started toward the stairs. "Let's check out the second floor."

The upper story with its eight guest rooms and three suites had multiple problems, chief of which was damage from several leaks in the roof over the years. Ceilings had fallen in several of the rooms, and mattresses had molded. Many of the furnishings were ruined, and evidence of mice having taken over the building was everywhere.

Two hours later, they locked the double doors of the main entrance and left the Lodge to drive back to the ranchhouse.

"It's a hell of a mess," Cade commented as they parked in front of the house and headed inside.

"Yeah, it is that," Zach agreed as he followed his brother down the hall to the empty kitchen.

They found the carafe filled with fresh coffee and a note from Mariah telling Cade she'd gone to town.

"The building's structurally sound," Zach continued when they sat at the table. "But if we want to restore and reopen the Lodge to guests, it's going to take a lot of work."

"And a lot of money," Cade added drily.

Zach shrugged. "That goes without saying. But then, in my experience, those two usually go hand in hand."

"So you're thinking of renovating the Lodge and re-opening it?" Cade asked, lifting his mug to drink.

"I have to crunch the numbers first, but…yeah, I think so," Zach answered slowly. "Over the years I've run into old friends of Mom and Dad's who used to stay at the Lodge. They all told me how much they loved coming to the Triple C and how sorry they were to hear about Mom's accident." He sipped his coffee, thinking about those conversations before continuing. "And every time, each one told me to let them know if the Lodge ever reopened because they'd be the first to reserve a room."

His eyes narrowed in thought. "I wonder if the old guest register is still in the office."

"If we could find it, you'd have a list of people to contact and maybe the rooms would all be booked before the Lodge opened again."

"Maybe," Zach agreed. "I don't know how long it would take to gut the building and renovate it." He took his cell phone from his pocket. "I need to make a few calls. First to Angela to see if she's had any luck looking for Eli and Brodie. Then I'll call my boss and let him know what's going on."

"Think he'll give you a leave of absence, or will you have to quit?" Cade asked.

Zach shrugged. "I freelance, and my contract doesn't have a set number of hours. He's used to me going off the standby list every now and then so I doubt he'll give me any trouble. Besides—" he flashed a smile "—we've known each other a long time. I don't expect any trouble."

"Good. What about financing?"

"I'll get a business loan, probably."

"You could sell Mom's mustang sculpture." Cade's deep voice was quiet. "All of her work has skyrocketed in value over the last twenty years. The sale price of the piece might be enough to cover the renovations."

"I thought about that." Zach met his brother's gaze. "I'll consider it if there's no other way. But until we know there's no other choice, I want it left on the wall at the Lodge. It feels right for it to be there—where Mom wanted it hung and where it's stayed all these years."

"Your call." Cade's voice was noncommittal, but his eyes held understanding and agreement.

Four hours later, Zach had finished crunching numbers and called his boss. When he hung up, he not only had an open-ended approval of leave on his contract duties, he also had a guarantee of financing from his boss's company.

Between helping Cade repair pasture fences, replace the brakes on a tractor and lining up contractors to work on the Lodge renovations, it was four days before Zach was back in Indian Springs. He'd worked long hours, accomplished a lot and missed too much sleep.

He hadn't been able to forget Cynthia Deacon, though, and when someone needed to make a trip to the feed store to pick up an engine part, Zach had instantly volunteered, hoping to run into the beautiful blonde.

Just as he finished loading the sacks of grain into the back of his truck, fate decided to take pity on him. He glanced across the street just as Cynthia stepped out of a café, pausing to put on a pair of dark-framed sunglasses. She wore a bright blue top that left her arms bare and a white skirt that hugged her hips and ended above her knees. Her long blond hair was loose, falling down her back past her shoulders. She looked better in person than she had in the dreams that haunted Zach's sleep.

Zach started across the street, halting to let a dusty pickup drive by before he jogged the rest of the way and stepped up on the curb.

"Hello." He was only a few feet from her when he spoke.

Cynthia immediately recognized the deep male voice drawling the greeting and she couldn't restrain the smile that curved her lips before looking over her shoulder. The corners of his mouth lifted in an answering smile that appeared to say he was as delighted to see her as she was to see him.

She turned and, with slow deliberation, let her gaze move from the top of the white Stetson that sat atop his black hair with the brim tugged low on his brow, down the length of his muscled body in white T-shirt and faded tight jeans to the toes of his black cowboy boots. "My, my, Mr. Coulter. You look like a cowboy."

His eyes sparkled with laughter but his voice was grave. "I am a cowboy, Ms. Deacon."

"Hmm." She lifted an eyebrow. "I thought you were a corporate shark."

He nodded. "I am—just taking a break for now." He nodded at the café behind her. "Can I buy you coffee? Soda? Chocolate cake?"

She narrowed her eyes at him. "What makes you think I like chocolate cake?"

Shock spread over his features. "You don't like chocolate cake?"

"I didn't say I don't, I'm just wondering why you assume that I do."

He cocked his head, fixing her with an interested stare. "I've never known a woman who doesn't like chocolate cake. On a scale of one to ten, seduction-wise, chocolate cake is right up there with roses."

She rolled her eyes, hiding a smile. "You're impossible." She turned on her heel and strolled away, window-shopping as she walked and well aware he prowled just behind her. "How are things out at the Triple C?" she asked, glancing sideways at him.

He shrugged, powerful muscles shifting under the white T-shirt. "Busy. I'm in town to pick up some parts for equipment we're rebuilding and sacks of grain at Miller's Feed."

"It's nice that you can take time away from work to stay and help your brother," Cynthia commented, lowering her sunglasses to look at him. "I'm sure your brothers will be glad you can stay. How long will you be here?"

"I'm not sure. We're still looking for my two younger brothers, so I'll be here at least until they make it home."

"You must have a very accommodating boss if he'll let you take an indefinite leave of absence," she commented, curious.

"My boss and I have an understanding," he said with a slow smile.

And what did that mean? she wondered. "What kind of work do you do—when you're not climbing mountains?" she asked aloud.

"I work for a capital venture firm in San Francisco. The CEO calls me in to analyze companies the firm has either bought or plans to buy. I spend a few weeks on-site and after assessing the potential problems tell him whether he should keep the company."

"You're a corporate hatchet man." She eyed him consideringly.

He winced. "That's not the term I like to use."

"What job description do you use?"

"Financial analyst," he said promptly.

She shook her head. "No, sorry, that's way too innocuous. I bet the people working at those companies think of you as a hatchet man."

He laughed. "You could be right. It's the nature of the job—nobody likes to be out of work."

"As I can certainly confirm," she said without thinking.

His gaze sharpened. "Are you unemployed?"

"Temporarily," she said with an offhand breeziness she wished was real. "But as it turns out, the timing was fortunate, since I had to come back to Indian Springs to take care of my great-uncle's estate."

"That was Nicholas Deacon?"

She tensed. "Yes, that's right. Did you know him?"

"No, can't say that I had the pleasure. Mariah mentioned the other day that you'd returned to settle Nicholas Deacon's estate." He looked at her, his green eyes warm. "I take it the two of you were close?"

"I adored him," Cynthia said. "I grew up in his house. He taught me to garden and play checkers, and showed me how to make a perfect pot roast." She smiled, aware her vision had gone misty. "He was a wonderful man. The best uncle ever." She lifted her sunglasses to brush her fingertips over her lashes, then drew a deep breath. "But he wouldn't want me to cry over him. Nicholas was a practical and pragmatic man. He'd tell me to get on with my life and not worry about him because he's with Min now. She was his wife," she added in explanation. "They loved to dance and they're probably waltzing all over heaven together, having a fabulous time."

"He sounds like a great guy," Zach commented, his deep voice gentle.

"He was. I wouldn't have survived childhood without

him." She slipped her sunglasses off to better view his reaction. "My mother is Natasha Deacon." She watched Zach's face but couldn't detect any change in expression. Either he already knew about her mother, whose dark-haired beauty and promiscuous lifestyle had gained her a notorious reputation in the county, or he hadn't heard the gossip about Natasha.

Zach merely nodded, his expression grave and non-judgmental. "I knew Natasha was Nicholas's niece, so I assumed there was a connection between you and her."

"Yes, well…" Cynthia sighed. "As I said, Nicholas was wonderful and I missed seeing him after I left for college."

"Where did you go to college?" he asked.

"Harvard—too far away to come home very often during school. I had scholarships, but I had to work during the summer so I didn't get to visit Nicholas then, either."

"I went to Berkeley," he told her. "What did you major in?"

Warmed by what seemed to be genuine interest, Cynthia smiled at him. "Business."

"And what have you been doing since college—working on Wall Street?" he asked, eyes gently teasing.

She shook her head. "No, I've been managing hotels—small boutique hotels. It's a great job and I've traveled a lot." She frowned. "But I'm currently unemployed and finding it's not as easy to find work in today's market."

Cynthia realized she'd said more than she'd planned to about her home life as a child. What was it about Zach that made her open up about subjects and her personal life that she never talked about with anyone else? "Listen to me, going on about myself and losing my great-uncle when you've lost your father recently, too. You must know exactly how I feel."

"Not really." His voice was cooler, bordering on caustic.

Startled, she looked at him, eyebrows lifting in surprise.

He shrugged. "I hadn't seen my father in more than a decade."

A horn honked on the street behind them, and they both turned. Grady Turner leaned out the passenger window of a passing truck, its bed fully-loaded with bales of hay.

"Hey, Cynthia—Zach."

They returned his greeting, and Cynthia waved.

When she looked back at Zach, his eyes were narrowed over her. "Are you and Grady Turner seeing each other?"

Startled, she felt her eyes widen. "You mean—like, dating?"

He nodded and she laughed, a peal of pure amusement.

"Goodness, no. I've known Grady since we were in kindergarten. He's just a friend."

"My brothers and I spent as much time as we could at the Turner ranch when we were growing up," Zach said. "All of us are good friends, but of the six Turner brothers, I guess I'm closer to Grady than the rest."

"He's a good guy," Cynthia said with affection. "Getting to see him more frequently is one of the perks of being back in Indian Springs."

"You know," Zach said, "I feel the same way."

They smiled at each other. The sense of being in perfect accord with another person was something Cynthia had rarely felt before. The connection surprised and startled her.

Zach Coulter was handsome, sexy and blatantly male, but she hadn't expected to feel a connection with him.

Suddenly realizing they'd been standing on the sidewalk talking for more than a few minutes, she glanced at her watch and gasped.

"I'm late for an appointment. I'm sorry to run off again, Zach, but I have to go."

Flustered, she caught a glimpse of his amused smile and his drawled farewell as she turned and hurried off down the street. When she pulled open the door to Jeanne Renee's Hair Salon a half block away, she looked back.

Just as before, he was still standing there, watching her.

She lifted a hand to wave and he nodded, touching the brim of his hat.

She stepped inside the salon, wishing she had stayed with him longer. And knowing she was much better off keeping her distance from a man like him.

Chapter Five

Not quite a week after talking to Zach Coulter outside the café on Main Street, Cynthia was on her front porch, sitting on a wicker love seat with her feet propped on the edge of the matching glass-topped coffee table in front of her. She bent over, stretching to reach her toes. With deft, practiced strokes, she used the tiny brush to apply a second coat of scarlet to her toenails. The red polish matched her favorite summer top, a loose cotton cami-sole with tiny spaghetti straps that she wore over white shorts in the balmy, mid-seventy-degree afternoon.

She leaned back, critically eyeing the bright color tipping her toes.

This is what my life has come to, she thought with a groan. *Spending the afternoon trying to paint my toe-nails without a single smudge.*

Sighing again, she gazed around at the yard. Where Cynthia sat, the porch was shaded by a thick lilac bush, and flower beds skirted the front and sides of the house. A brick walkway ran from the foot of the wide porch steps directly to a gate in the picket fence that let out onto the sidewalk and street. Cynthia's convertible was parked in the drive just beyond the end of the porch. She'd left it there earlier when she came home from the pharmacy after purchasing the new scarlet nail polish she was currently applying so meticulously to her toenails.

A girl needed a pedicure now and then. Especially when she was doing her best *not* to think about a man like Zach Coulter.

She frowned.

Earlier this morning, she'd stood in line behind two older women at the grocery store and she couldn't help but overhear as they spent long moments speculating about Zach and his brothers.

As Cynthia well remembered, this kind of endless discussion about the Coulter boys was a popular pastime for the folks in Indian Springs. She'd been a freshman in high school when the youngest, Eli, was a senior. He and his three older brothers had been wild, and wildly popular. In contrast, she'd been quiet, studious and not the slightest bit socially active, although she'd had a few close friends. She hadn't attended her high school prom nor any of the parties after graduation.

In fact, she mused, she wasn't surprised that Zach didn't remember her. After her mother accused her of inviting his attentions when Natasha's boyfriend attacked her, she'd taken to wearing clothing that concealed her budding shape. As a teenager, she'd done everything possible to fade into the background and remain inconspicuous. She certainly remembered Zach and his brothers, though—their bigger-than-life personalities, their reputations, their coal-black hair, green eyes, broad-shouldered bodies and sheer male power. It was a wonder the female population of Indian Springs had survived the excitement and heart palpitations the Coulter boys had caused just by their existence.

She plucked the cotton balls from between her toes, tossed them into the empty pharmacy bag and walked down the porch steps to the water spigot at the corner of the house. Twisting the handle, she filled a metal watering can and carried it back onto the porch to water the pots and hanging baskets filled with red and white geraniums and trailing green ivy. Toes curling against the cool boards of the floor, she bent to reach a terra-cotta pot filled with herbs, the plants still small green shoots only inches above the black dirt.

"Good morning."

The deep male drawl had her spinning around. Water from the can splashed her toes. Zach walked toward her up the walkway and behind him, a newer model black pickup truck was parked at her curb.

"Hello." She didn't move, staring at him. She hadn't heard his truck and she briefly wondered if merely thinking about him had conjured him up out of thin air. "What brings you out this morning?"

"Actually, I came into town to see you." He mounted the shallow steps.

Cynthia stepped back, unconsciously giving way before she realized she was doing so and stopped abruptly. Pleased though she was to see him, she couldn't help wondering why he was here. She tried to ignore the heated rush of blood as her heart beat faster.

"I see." She didn't, not really, but nonetheless, gestured to the corner of the porch where two wicker armchairs sat at right angles to the love seat. "I was about to have coffee. Would you like some?"

"Thanks." He followed her across the porch, waiting until she settled onto the love seat before dropping into an armchair. He took off his white Stetson and set it on the empty seat of the second wicker chair, raking his fingers through his hair.

"What's it like being home again after so much time away?" she asked, willing her fingers not to tremble as she poured coffee into mugs and handed one to him. She'd brought the carafe out earlier, knowing she'd want a cup before long.

He leaned forward to take the cup from her hands, his fingers brushing hers.

Even the small contact sizzled along her nerve endings. It was all she could do not to snatch her hand away from his. Instead, she calmly filled a mug for herself and sat back, sipping her coffee while trying not to stare.

In the days since they'd talked briefly outside the cafe on Main Street, Cynthia had repeatedly told herself Zach couldn't possibly have looked as good as she remembered—but she'd been fooling herself. The reality was better than her memory—and her memory had been pretty spectacular.

He sat relaxed in the white chair, the blue mug held loosely in one hand, his right ankle resting on the knee of his bent left leg. His black hair gleamed in the sunlight, his tanned skin dark against the stark white of a

Western shirt that fastened with black pearl snaps down the front. His long sleeves were rolled up to reveal the powerful muscles of his forearms, the shirttails tucked into the belted waistband of faded jeans that faithfully hugged the heavy muscles of his thighs.

He looked wholly male sitting in the feminine white wicker chair with its floral rose cushions. And yet, he seemed totally relaxed and comfortable.

No wonder the women in Indian Springs gossip about him, Cynthia thought. *Just looking at him is better than eating a gallon of toffee-caramel ice cream.*

"To be honest, I'm not sure I can tell you."

"Hmm?" She scrambled blankly for a second, trying to remember what she'd asked him. Then memory kicked in. Oh, yes, she'd wondered how it felt to be home. "Really? Why not?"

"Sometimes it's as if I left town only yesterday and other times, I feel like a stranger." He shrugged. "Hard to explain."

"I've felt like that a few times since I've been home," she told him. The pull of sexual tension eased a fraction as sympathy for their shared experience flooded her.

"Yeah?" He lifted an eyebrow, waiting expectantly.

"When I feel as if I left only yesterday it's usually when I'm doing something I loved as a child." She pointed at the flower beds along the picket fence. "Like raking the flower beds. I used to do that every spring, summer and fall with my Uncle Nicholas and the memory is still so clear that for a moment yesterday, I was disoriented. I actually felt a little dizzy and unbalanced for a few seconds."

"That's it, exactly," he agreed. "Although I haven't

felt dizzy—nothing physical, just the odd moment of feeling as if I'm caught in a time warp." He eyed her quizzically. "How long since you were home last?"

"I visited my uncle about four months ago but I was here only for a few days." Cynthia let her gaze move slowly over the porch and the sunlit yard beyond. "Everything was covered in snow then," she said with a sigh. "And Nicholas was drawing up sketches for the flower beds. He wanted to put in a perennial border along the fence between our yard and Mrs. Riley's next door. He had seed catalogs stacked on the dining room table."

"What happened?"

"He was sitting in his chair in the living room and apparently had a massive heart attack. The doctors told me he probably never knew what was happening."

"That's not a bad way to go," Zach commented, his voice gentle.

"Yes, he had ninety-two wonderful years of living and he was healthy, active and happy right up until the end." Cynthia realized her eyes were damp. She brushed her fingertips over her lashes before looking back at him. "What about your father?"

"He had lung cancer," Zach told her, the gentleness gone from his features and replaced by an odd lack of expression. "Apparently, he was ill for some time."

"And no one let you know?" Cynthia asked, surprised. Once again, a feeling of kinship filled her.

"I didn't keep in touch after I left the Triple C," he told her. "I doubt anyone knew how to contact me—or any of my brothers."

"I'm sorry." Sympathy had her instinctively leaning forward.

72   *THE VIRGIN AND ZACH COULTER*

"Don't be," he told her. "We weren't exactly the perfect family. In fact—" his mouth twisted with derision "—I'd say we're pretty much the poster family for dysfunction."

Cynthia frowned. "I'm sorry, I didn't mean to dredge up bad memories." She'd heard her mother, neighbors and school friends gossip about Joseph Coulter's drinking and his sons' wild ways, but the details had always been vague.

"You didn't." He shook his head. "That's all water under the bridge. Over and done with." He sat forward, both feet on the floor, his forearms propped on his thighs and hands cradling the blue coffee mug. "But my family and their history at the Triple C does have something to do with the reason I came here this morning."

"What's that?" Puzzled, she searched his features but couldn't read a trace of sadness or regret for his father's passing.

"You told me you have experience in managing boutique hotels."

"That's true." *Although,* she thought wryly, *my career is pretty much at a standstill at the moment.*

"I'm renovating and reopening the Coulter Lodge. I'd like you to come to work for me."

Cynthia was speechless. A job offer was the last thing she'd had on her mind when she'd seen him striding up her sidewalk.

"I'm at the planning stage, but speed is crucial," he went on. "I need someone who understands the business and can come on board immediately. Are you interested?"

"I'm always interested in job offers," Cynthia said,

trying to consider all the aspects. "But I can't give you an answer until I know more about it."

"Makes sense." He nodded as if approving. "Since you grew up in Indian Springs, I'm assuming you know a bit about the Coulter Lodge but I'll start with a brief history. The Lodge was my mother's idea. Dad was an expert fly fisherman—some said he was gifted—and he loved to hunt quail and pheasant. He had so many friends visiting to join him that Mom told him he should open a business. So he did. She designed the Lodge, he had it built and hired a crew to run it.

"During the ten or so years it was open, guests came from around the world to take fly-fishing lessons from Dad and go hunting with their friends." Zach paused to take a drink of coffee. "When my mother died, Dad closed up the Lodge, and that was twenty-three years ago. It remained sealed until last week when Cade and I went in."

He fell silent, the clipped words and brief sentences delivered in an unemotional tone as if he were reading the history of strangers from a book page. Once again, however, his eyes were alive with emotions.

"What did you find inside?" Cynthia prompted, enthralled by the bare-bones story and the human tragedy behind it that she suspected went much deeper.

"Lots of dust, cobwebs, water damage upstairs," he told her. "The bones of the structure are solid, but it's going to take a lot of work before it can be reopened."

"Are all the furnishings ruined?"

He shook his head. "Not everything. A few of the bedsteads and antique oak dressers, washstands, etcetera, are fine. But nearly all of the furniture will have to be replaced because of damage from the mice, raccoons and water. And all of the mattresses, drapes, bedding and any upholstered furniture will have to be tossed out."

"It must have been eerie," she mused, "walking into a building that's been sealed for so long."

"It was a little odd," he confirmed, but the inflection was back in his voice and a small smile lifted the corner of his mouth.

Cynthia drew her attention away from the curve of his lips and tried to focus on the details of his job offer. "You said you want a manager on board immediately, but clearly it's going to be some time before there's a hotel to run. What short-term duties would the position have?"

"My goal is to have the Lodge open, filled to capacity and generating income as soon as possible. I've hired a crew and we'll start tearing out drywall day after tomorrow but I need a person who's knowledgeable about the business immediately. Someone who can handle the details of finding and hiring an advertising firm, choosing and replacing the necessary furnishings—generally overseeing the entire operation."

"What salary are you offering?"

The dollar figure he named stunned Cynthia, although she'd braced herself not to react. It was more than twice what her last job had paid and in addition, she wouldn't have to leave Nicholas's house. The surge of elation was tempered with caution, however. Before she allowed herself to become involved, she needed to know the ground rules.

"However, until the hotel is open and generates

income, you'd need to be willing to be creative about compensation. Because although I have a venture capitalist funding the project, the capital outlay for the building renovation alone is going to be huge."

"The salary is certainly competitive," she said calmly. "I'm not averse to a creative compensation package if the terms are right. And the job sounds like a challenge, which is always a plus for me. But…" She drew a breath. "I'm going to be blunt with you, Zach. I may be misreading the situation, but I sense a personal…something… between us. Am I wrong?"

The look in his eyes grew heated. "No, you're not wrong."

She leaned forward and set her mug on the glass-topped table between them before clasping her hands together and resting them on her knees, her back ramrod straight as she met his gaze. "That concerns me. Although I wouldn't normally discuss this with a prospective employer, I think I have to tell you that the reason I left my last position was…well, I was being sexually harassed by the hotel owner."

His eyes narrowed, his big body going tense. "What happened?"

"He felt my job included my going to bed with him. I disagreed," she said coolly. "I walked out. I doubt he'll give me a good reference, should you ask."

"Hell." Zach set his mug down on the table with a snap. "The bastard should be shot."

His instant anger was a relief. "I take it that means you don't hold the same view?" she asked mildly.

"Of course not." He looked insulted. "What do you take me for?"

"Truthfully?" She considered him for a moment. "I can't imagine you'd need to threaten a woman to get her into bed with you," she said candidly.

His eyes lit with amusement, chasing away the remnants of anger. "No, ma'am," he drawled. "I don't remember a time when I had to resort to threats."

"Nevertheless," she said repressively, trying not to be charmed by his smile. "That still leaves the question of what appears to be an attraction between us. I'm not comfortable accepting your offer until the issue is resolved. Particularly after what happened at my last job," she added firmly.

"I understand." His eyes narrowed over her. "Cards on the table?"

"Please." She nodded.

"I want you," he said bluntly, his gaze holding hers. "If you said yes, I'd take you to bed and keep you there for hours, probably until tomorrow, maybe longer. But I don't think you're ready for that and besides, I need your expertise at the Lodge."

Cynthia ignored the rush of awareness that raced along her nerves, clenched her abdomen and tightened her thighs. "I'd like to help bring the Lodge back to life. But I need your promise that you won't use your position as my employer to pressure me for anything beyond a business relationship."

"Pressure you?" He stared at her, eyelashes lowering as he focused intently on her mouth before his gaze returned to hers. "I can promise I'll treat you with all the respect due your profession—and that I won't make passes while we're working."

Just as relief flooded her, he added "Unless you make it clear you want me to."

"I thought we were being honest," she said heatedly.

"I'm being as honest as it's possible for me to be in this situation—but I'm also being practical," he said. "I'd never force my attentions on an unwilling woman. But I don't think for a minute that we're going to be able to ignore the heat between us forever. Sooner or later, we're going to give in. It's inevitable."

"You have an ego the size of Mount Rushmore," she snapped, feeling her cheeks heat. "But as long as you can promise you won't force me to cooperate, there won't be a problem."

"You sound convinced."

"I am." She nodded, a brief decisive move of her head to underline her words.

He stood and stepped over the coffee table.

"What are you...?" Cynthia tipped her head back to look up at him but before she could finish her sentence, he bent and picked her up, then sat down on the love seat with her on his lap.

It happened so fast she had no time to gather her wits before he bent his head and kissed her.

She caught her breath, startled, as his warm mouth covered hers. For long moments, his lips plundered hers, changing pressure from firm to soft as he coaxed her to respond. He stroked the tip of his tongue over the seam of her lips. She wanted, needed, craved, more and she let him in. He rewarded her by cradling the back of her head in the palm of his hand and tilting her face up to his to seal their mouths together. She forgot to breathe as her heart raced faster and heat poured through her body, melting her against him, while his lips seduced and his tongue lured and teased hers. By the time he lifted his head, she was breathless and fighting the urge to pull his mouth back to hers.

"Sometimes a demonstration is best," he said, his breathing ragged. "Are you still convinced pretending the heat between us doesn't exist will make it go away?"

The rasping sound of his deep voice rubbed over Cynthia's nerves, stirring a yearning need she suspected was better left sleeping.

"This is exactly the sort of thing I insist you not do," she told him, her voice not altogether steady as she pushed away from him and stood. Her legs felt distinctly wobbly, she realized with dismay.

Zach rose to stand beside her. "All right. I promise not to repeat this, unless you ask me to," he told her.

"Then we don't have a problem." She narrowed her eyes over him. "Do we?"

"No problem—"

"Good."

"But sooner or later, we're going to end up doing more than kissing. It's inevitable."

Cynthia felt like pulling her hair. "You're incredibly single-minded."

"No. I just recognize sexual tension when I feel it— and you and I have it in spades."

"We're adults, not teenagers who can't control their raging hormones. We'll deal with it."

"We'll deal with it," he agreed. His expression was solemn but his eyes laughed at her.

Cynthia decided to leave well enough alone.

"Before I accept the job, I think I should see the Lodge for myself," she said briskly, determined not to think about how close he stood, the faint smell of aftershave and warm male that she drew in with each breath and the ridiculous way her fingers itched with the need to reach out and test the warmth of his cheek. She couldn't help but wonder how the faint shadow of beard stubble would feel beneath her sensitive fingertips. She'd loved the slight roughness against her cheek when they kissed.

"That's probably a good idea. I'd prefer you have a clear grasp of the scope of the project before you commit." He bent to pick up his Stetson and settled it on his head, tugging the brim down over his brow. "Why don't you come out to the Triple C around eight o'clock tomorrow morning? I'll drive you down to the Lodge."

"I'll be there," she said.

"Good." He smiled at her. "Wear clothes you don't mind getting dirty. There's dust and cobwebs inches deep over everything."

"Thanks for the warning."

"You're welcome. See you tomorrow." He touched the brim of his hat and left the porch.

Moments later, he drove away, the black truck disappearing down the street.

Cynthia released the breath she hadn't realized she'd been holding and collapsed onto the wicker love seat.

Was she really considering working with him? Was there even a remote chance she could be around him on a daily basis without begging him to kiss her again?

Chapter Six

As she ate an early dinner that evening, her thoughts kept returning to those too-brief moments with Zach. Heat flooded her and the memory of his mouth on hers sizzled along her nerve endings.

She'd been kissed before, many times—but never quite so thoroughly. Zach was a man who clearly enjoyed kissing and he took his time, as if savoring the press and taste of her mouth under his. She couldn't help but wonder what else he did with that same, slow attention to detail.

She shivered and wrapped her arms over her midriff, wondering how many women he'd kissed to develop that kind of bone-melting expertise. Dozens, at least. Hundreds? Possibly.

And that, she realized with sudden insight, *is exactly why I'll be safe working with him.*

Because no man with his experience would want an

inexperienced woman in his bed—and Cynthia's experience was zero.

She'd lied to him when she said she had no worries about her ability to refuse him. The truth was, when he'd picked her up, settled her on his lap, wrapped her in his arms with his mouth on hers, she'd been in real danger of following wherever he chose to lead.

She hadn't stopped him—Zach was the one who had pulled back. And although she might deny it to anyone else, the truth was she hadn't wanted him to release her.

If, by chance, things did grow heated between them again, she'd have to remember to tell him no *before* he kissed her, since she apparently lost all ability to think when he got too close.

And if she felt the attraction was growing dangerously near to irresistible, she'd have to confess her secret.

She'd never slept with anyone. In a world where virginity seemed to be increasingly rare, Cynthia had held on to hers with the same strength of will that marked her drive to earn top grades in school from elementary through graduation from Harvard.

Looking back, she'd felt she had valid, compelling reasons for doing so. Her mother bounced from one love affair to the next while Cynthia was growing up—her many affairs made her the focus of local gossip and earned her a notorious reputation.

Natasha Deacon had been unwed when she gave birth to Cynthia at seventeen and although Cynthia had repeatedly asked, she'd never learned who her father was. Her mother refused to say and she'd finally stopped asking. She had Nicholas as a father figure and the gentle older man was wonderful.

The fallout for being the daughter of the most scandalous woman in the county, however, was impossible to avoid. Although she'd been a shy, bookish child, by the time Cynthia was in junior high, boys assumed she would be as promiscuous as her mother. Mortified by the attention gained by her developing curves, she'd taken to wearing her clothes a size too big to conceal her body. But it was the unwanted attention from one of her mother's boyfriends when Cynthia was twelve that made her retreat from any interaction with boys.

With the exception of Grady Turner, who continued to treat her just as he had since he'd sat in the desk behind her in third grade, she ignored the male half of the high school population. By the time she arrived at Harvard, the habits she'd developed earlier were so ingrained she barely knew she froze men out of her life.

The end result was that Cynthia remained a virgin at the age of twenty-eight. And though she hadn't consciously planned to wait so long, the trauma at age twelve had effectively insulated her until the rush of raging teenage hormones had leveled out. Then it became an issue of meeting a man she really wanted to be intimate with. Not to mention the fact that she had to reveal she was a total novice in the bedroom.

In a world saturated with magazine articles about new and inventive ways to please your man, and media that seemed to declare everyone over the age of thirteen was having sex, Cynthia couldn't help but think her lack of experience was a huge hurdle.

Although she'd hoped several men she'd dated would

be the one to solve her problem, the relationships had fizzled and she'd moved on, still a virgin. Over the past year, she'd seriously been considering how, when, where and with whom to change her status. Unfortunately, the solution still hinged on finding the right man and so far, she'd had no luck.

And then Zach Coulter had walked into her life.

Now she couldn't help but wonder, and wish, that she'd met him when she was a teenager, and that her mother's boyfriend hadn't been drinking too much and that she hadn't been alone that night.

Maybe Zach would have been her first lover. Of course, he would have left town, and her, but still...

She sighed. Too late for wishes. She couldn't undo the past. She couldn't imagine having to confess she was still completely inexperienced. She cringed just thinking about it. So she could only hope Zach was wrong and that their attraction would fizzle out after they'd worked together for a while. Because working at the Lodge meant she could stay in Indian Springs, live in Nicholas's lovely home and settle down. And although she suspected having an affair with Zach would be better than her wildest dreams, he would surely quickly grow bored with her inexperience.

She'd worked with men and women who were ex-lovers and knew the situation could be an emotionally explosive minefield.

No, she thought, if she wanted to work at the Lodge, she had to stay out of Zach's bed.

The men in her past who'd been interested in her had eventually given up after she'd repeatedly ignored their advances. Granted, Zach seemed much more determined but still, sooner or later, she was sure he'd give up and move on to more interesting game.

Which was a shame, she thought wistfully, because she would really love to have more of those toe curling kisses.

She finished eating, then tidied the kitchen before settling into the living room to boot up her laptop and research the history of the Coulter Lodge on the internet.

Later that evening, after she showered, donned pajamas and settled in with a bowl of popcorn to watch an old Alfred Hitchcock movie on TV, Cynthia considered the lack of information she'd found online about the Coulters.

It was as if the Coulter family had dropped off the face of the earth after Melanie Coulter's death. Prior to the date of the tragic accident that took her life, the newspaper archives were filled with articles about the rising star of the art world. Melanie's silver, copper and bronze work was nationally acclaimed. She'd won a coveted award and photos of her at the ceremony in New York City which she'd attended with her husband and four sons showed a happy, loving family. The Coulter Lodge was mentioned in articles featuring celebrities in the entertainment industry as well as the financial world, politics and American blueblood society.

There were numerous articles about Zach's mother's death and follow-up pieces reporting the media lockout by her grieving husband. But those slowed to a trickle and within a few months, stopped altogether.

The only references Cynthia could find to the family after that first year following Melanie Coulter's death were related to art auctions. Even after she was gone, Melanie's work continued to gain in value, the price of the few pieces on the market skyrocketing each time one came up for sale as collectors snapped up the sculptures.

But the family was silent—and if Melanie had left unfinished pieces in her studio at the Triple C, no one would confirm, although art historians continued to speculate.

I wish I'd asked Zach if the Lodge had any of his mother's artwork, Cynthia thought. The photos she'd viewed courtesy of the internet had been stunning. The sculptures of mustangs were especially vivid and so lifelike Cynthia almost felt they could step out of her laptop and thunder away.

The phone rang, startling her. She hastily wiped the popcorn salt from her fingers, muted the television and grabbed the phone from the table next to the sofa.

"Hello?"

"What took you so long to answer?"

Cynthia nearly groaned out loud. How like her mother to not bother saying hello before criticizing. "I'm eating popcorn and didn't want to get salt and butter on the phone." Her mother rarely called but when she did, it was nearly always because she wanted something. Usually that something was money.

"I don't know why you'd care," Natasha Deacon said dismissively. "Now that Nicholas isn't there to nitpick over every little fingerprint, I'd think you'd relax a little."

"I like Nicholas's neatness. And I love his house. The

trees are leafed out and the flowers are blooming. It's lovely here."

"I'm sure," Natasha said impatiently. "I don't know why you like that old house so much. Listen, I don't have long to talk before Roger comes back…"

"Who's Roger?" Cynthia asked, trying to put a face with the name.

"You haven't met him," her mother told her. "We've only been together for five months."

"What happened to the one before that… George, I think his name was?"

"For goodness' sake, Cynthia, try to keep up." Natasha was clearly exasperated. "I broke up with George over a year ago."

"Ah." Cynthia didn't know what to say. Her mother cycled through men too frequently for her to keep track. *I need a score card,* she thought wryly.

"The point is," Natasha went on as if Cynthia hadn't spoken. "Roger is being difficult and I need to move out, get my own apartment and start a new life."

This time, Cynthia couldn't catch the groan before it escaped her lips. "Natasha, not again."

"Don't judge me, Cynthia." Natasha's voice was sharp. "I only need to borrow enough for first and last months' rent. I'll pay you back."

"I'm sure you would, Natasha, but unfortunately, I can't swing a loan right now."

"Don't be ridiculous. You save money from your pay-check every week. You always have. How long are you staying in Indian Springs?"

"I don't know," Cynthia replied cautiously.

"Why don't you know? How long did you tell your boss you'd be gone?"

"I no longer have a boss. I quit my job in Palm Springs."

The dead silence on the phone was testimony to the unprecedented news.

"That's not possible. Unless you took a better position somewhere else."

"No, actually, I just walked out."

"Why on earth would you leave a job at a posh hotel in Palm Springs?" Natasha demanded, disbelief carrying clearly over the line. "I wanted to visit you there this winter. It was the perfect place to get away from Montana's cold and snow in February."

"I left because the head of the company expected me to sleep with him. As I remember, he told me it was one of the 'perks of the job.' I disagreed. And I left."

"That's it? That's the reason you left—because the boss wanted to sleep with you?"

"That's pretty much it, yes." Cynthia braced herself for the tirade she knew was sure to follow her confirmation.

"When are you going to grow up and start living in the real world, Cynthia? How many times have I told you this world is ruled by men and a woman has to do whatever's necessary to get ahead?"

"More times than I can count," Cynthia said, stifling a sigh.

"I can't believe you left a job that paid so well and was in such a perfect vacation spot." Natasha sounded seriously miffed. "It's a good thing you always have a healthy savings account—which brings us back to the important issue here. I need you to send me a check."

"Mother…"

"How many times have I told you not to call me that?" Natasha's voice rang with exasperation. "I'm much too young to have a daughter your age and I'm tired of explaining to people that I was barely a child myself when you were born."

Cynthia rolled her eyes. "If you want to be called Natasha, I can certainly do that. For a moment there, I forgot the rules of our relationship."

"Don't be sarcastic," Natasha said sharply.

"Of course not. However," Cynthia said briskly, before her mother had a chance to argue, "I truly don't have any cash. My savings are tied up in IRA accounts, which will take some time to move from my last employer. So at the moment, I'm basically broke." She wasn't lying—not exactly, she thought. She did have cash in a savings account, but until she went back to work, the funds would have to cover her living expenses.

"This is extremely inconvenient for me, Cynthia." Natasha didn't bother to hide her frustration and annoyance. "I was counting on your help. You're the only family I have now that Nicholas is gone and we need to be able to rely on each other."

"I'm sorry, Natasha." Cynthia couldn't help reflecting that the sentiment had always been a one-way street for her mother—Natasha expected any request for assistance from her to be acknowledged and complied with instantly. But somehow, Natasha was never able to reciprocate since she was always too busy, or too far away, or much too needed elsewhere.

"I suppose I could stay with you at Nicholas's house if I absolutely had to," Natasha went on.

Cynthia's stomach clenched. "Of course you could," she said carefully.

"I'll have to review my options here," her mother said. "I'll let you know what I decide."

"Perhaps things will work out with Raymond," Cynthia said, fervently hoping they would.

"Roger. His name is Roger. Honestly, Cynthia, do you ever listen to anything I say?" Natasha demanded waspishly.

"I'm sorry. Roger."

"I have to go. I think I hear Roger's car in the drive. I'll keep in touch."

And she hung up without saying goodbye.

Cynthia set the receiver back in its cradle before she rubbed her temples where a dull headache was beginning to grow.

Natasha never changed. She was totally self-centered and incapable of seeing anything beyond herself. And she never took it well when Cynthia declined to cooperate in one of her plans.

She'd lost track of the number of times Natasha had needed to borrow first and last months' rent to leave a man. Cynthia couldn't imagine how her mother managed to fall in love several times a year. Each time, she swore that this time she'd found the perfect mate, time after time, year after year.

When she was younger, Cynthia had expected her mother to eventually realize that perhaps the one perfect man she kept looking for might not exist. But Natasha never seemed to reach that rational conclusion, despite so many failed live-in relationships and male friends that Cynthia had lost track of the names long, long ago.

She rose and went into the kitchen, returning with a glass of wine. Determinedly, she turned up the volume on the movie and tried to forget Natasha and her current problems.

By the time she switched off the television and headed for bed, Alfred Hitchcock's brilliant murder mystery had thoroughly distracted her from her earlier worries.

She laid out clothes for the following morning, and as she got into bed, the upsetting conversation with her mother was forgotten. Zach Coulter's green eyes drifted into her mind, the sensation of his lips against hers making her smile as she fell asleep.

Chapter Seven

The following morning, Cynthia left the house dressed in jeans, boots and a turquoise scooped-neck T-shirt under a gray zip-up hoodie. She'd caught her hair up in a high ponytail to keep it out of her way. Sunglasses protected her eyes from the early sun that was already warming the sage-dotted pastures. She turned off the highway, drove beneath the welded arch that spelled out Coulter Cattle Company and followed the recently graded and graveled ranch road until it ended in a wide ranch yard at the Triple C headquarters.

Recognizing the black pickup truck parked in front of the house as the one Zach had driven yesterday, she nosed her convertible next to the truck and got out, glancing around at the buildings.

Several people stood at the corral next to the barn.

"Cynthia," Zach called, beckoning to her.

She waved in response and started across the graveled

space between the house and the corral. As she neared, she recognized Mariah Jones from the Indian Springs Café, belatedly remembering she was engaged to Zach's older brother. The tall, black-haired man at her side looked so much like Zach that Cynthia knew he must be Cade Coulter.

Inside the corral, a teenaged boy sat easily atop a beautiful black horse.

"Good morning," she said as she drew near.

"Mornin'," Zach answered.

He swept her with a slow once-over that had her cheeks heating.

"Hi, Mariah," she said calmly, smiling at the blonde woman.

"You two know each other?" Zach asked.

"I met her at the café," Cynthia told him.

"Of course," he answered. "I should have guessed. Mariah knows everyone in the county because sooner or later, they all show up at the café. Her boss makes the best pies in Montana."

"That's true." Mariah laughed. "Good morning, Cynthia. Have you met Cade?"

"No, I don't believe I have."

"Nice to meet you, Cynthia," Cade said politely, his voice as deep as Zach's.

But unlike Zach's, Cade's voice didn't make her shiver with awareness.

"I hear you and Zach are looking over the Lodge today," Cade added.

She nodded. "I understand there's quite a lot of work to be done."

"That's the understatement of the year," Mariah put

in with a grimace. "But if anyone can restore it to its former grandeur, it's Zach."

"And if I'm lucky, I'll talk Cynthia into joining the cause," Zach said. "Ready to go?"

"Yes, whenever you are," she told him.

He took her elbow and turned her toward his truck. "We'll see you all later," he said over his shoulder as they walked away.

"Who's the young man on the horse?" she asked him as she latched her seat belt moments later.

"You mean J.T.? Sorry, I should have introduced you. He and Pete work here." Zach shifted the truck into gear and they left the ranch yard, following the gravel road past the big barn and the cabin that now belonged to Mariah. Then the road curved to follow the creek bank for a half mile to reach the Lodge.

"As I told you yesterday," Zach said when the Lodge came into view, "Dad built the Lodge based on Mom's designs. She wanted a mountain lodge constructed of big heavy logs with steep peaked roofs."

Cynthia drew in a quick breath, her gaze studying the building. The two-story structure was solid but somehow graceful. What must have once been a bright red metal roof had faded to rose and the big logs that made up the outer walls were aged to a mellow gold from exposure to weather. The deep porches that edged the front and three sides were welcoming despite the piles of boards stacked at intervals along the length and the covering of dust and cobwebs darkening the big windows.

Zach parked and he and Cynthia left the truck, climbing the shallow, wide steps to cross the porch and reach the front door.

"The windows and doors had lumber nailed over them. That's where the piles of wood came from." Zach pointed at the planks stacked at intervals along the porch. "Cade and I ripped them off last week so we could get inside."

"Did anyone ever break in over the years?" Cynthia asked with curiosity.

"Cade said there was an attempt since he's been home but he thought it was probably kids being curious and not a serious attempt at theft. J.T. came along and scared them off so they didn't actually get inside." Zach pulled a key ring from his pocket and slid the key into the hole with only minimal jiggling; it turned with a faint squeal. "I have to oil this lock," he commented as he shoved the door inward and stepped aside, waving Cynthia ahead of him.

She complied and halted abruptly just over the threshold.

Zach joined her, standing silently at her side as she swept her gaze over the big lobby.

Sunlight slanted through the open door behind them, throwing a bar of gold across the dust-covered wooden floor. Cobwebs hung from the wagon-wheel chandeliers at both ends of the long room and festooned the ironwork sconces along the walls. Dust lay inches deep on the wood and leather sofas and chairs, piled atop end tables and lampshades, and layered along the upper curve of logs that made up the walls.

At first, all Cynthia saw was the dust. But as she moved to walk farther into the lobby, she realized mice had used the upholstered furniture for beds. Stuffing poked out of the corners of sofa cushions and was strewn over the floor beneath. One corner of the thick Oriental carpet under her feet was shredded as if it had been chewed.

"That couldn't have been mice," she commented, pointing at the corner of the rug.

"No." Zach looked around. "I suspect raccoons broke in. The damage to some of the furniture looks like their work."

"Oh, my." Cynthia caught her breath, staring in amazement at the wall over the long reception counter. "Is the sculpture one of your mother's?"

Beneath a layer of dust and tarnish, a four foot tall, six foot long silver, copper and brass sculpture of mustangs in full gallop dominated the heavy log wall. Even covered in dirt, the horses seemed alive and ready to leap from the wall to race across the room. The breathtaking piece was vivid testimony to the depth and breadth of Melanie Coulter's incredible talent. Due to her research, Cynthia knew Zach's mother had been on the cusp of fully realizing her potential as an artist when the tragic accident took her life. She'd fallen while playing with her four sons in the creek, struck her head on a half-submerged rock and died within a week.

And apparently, Joseph Coulter had never recovered from her death. He'd sealed up her art studio, this Lodge she'd designed and loved, and a warehouse holding her collections of Western memorabilia.

"Yes, that's Mom's work." Zach's voice was devoid of emotion. "The horses are Kiger mustangs—she bred and raised a herd of them. She used them often as subjects for her art—she loved horses. After she died, Dad rode out early one morning, leading Mom's favorite saddlehorse. He returned hours later, without the mare. I always assumed he shot her but Dad wouldn't discuss it, so no one knows what he did with her."

"That's terrible." Cynthia didn't know what else to say. She guessed Zach must have been around eleven years old when his mother died. The articles Cynthia had read online speculated that Joseph Coulter had gone mad with grief. From the few comments Zach had made about his father and mother, she suspected the speculation might have been too close to the truth.

She turned in a slow circle, her gaze sliding over the lobby interior, amazed that until Zach removed the boards and entered, it would have been more than twenty-three years since anyone had set foot inside the lobby.

She shook her head and glanced sideways at Zach. "Given how long it's been since anyone's been inside, the condition doesn't seem that terrible."

Zach nodded slowly, his gaze sweeping the ceiling. "Yeah, I admit, I was surprised the damage wasn't worse down here." He pointed at a stain on the ceiling in the back corner. "The second floor didn't fare as well, though. You can see where water leaked through from the damage upstairs." He gestured toward the stairs. "Let's go up and I'll show you."

The upper story with its rooms and suites had multiple problems, chief of which was water damage from several leaks in the roof over the years. In several of the rooms, ceilings had fallen in, wood furnishings were warped and stained, and evidence of mice was everywhere. Several of the rooms were also ransacked, the damage consistent with a raccoon invasion. Cute though Cynthia thought they were, the animals could be incredibly destructive.

Two hours later, Zach locked the doors behind them and they left the Lodge to drive back to the ranch house, where they found a carafe filled with fresh coffee in the kitchen and a note from Mariah telling them she and Cade had gone into town.

"The Lodge is structurally sound," Zach continued when they sat at the table. "But as you say, the inside is a wreck. It's going to take a lot of work to restore it to the point where we can reopen it to guests again."

"And a lot of money," Cynthia added.

Zach shrugged. "That goes without saying. But in my experience, those two usually go hand in hand."

"Have you lined up financing?" she asked, accepting a mug from him. When their fingers brushed, she felt the quick zap of electricity she'd felt before, and her cheeks heated with awareness.

"Yes. My boss practically twisted my arm to give him the project." Zach shook his head, a slow smile tilting the corners of his mouth. "I warned him this is Montana, not San Francisco, but he said he believed in my gut instinct about the Lodge."

"And what does your gut tell you?" Cynthia asked, eyeing him curiously over the rim of her cup. His eyes were alive with energy, warming as his gaze focused on her mouth for a heart-stopping, intent moment.

"That it can be just as big a draw in the future as it was in the past," he told her with conviction. "I was at a conference in L.A. a few years ago and ran into an old friend of my parents. He's a movie executive and said he used to stay at the Lodge several times a year with his friends. They'd fly up from L.A. to take fly-fishing lessons from Dad in the summer and come back in the fall to hunt pheasant and grouse. He told me several times how much they loved coming here and how sorry they all were to hear about Mom's accident." He paused and sipped his coffee, his eyes going unfocused for a moment as if he were remembering the older man's words. Then his gaze sharpened once more. "And he told me to let him know if Dad ever decided to reopen the Lodge, so he could be the first returning guest. I think Angela still has his card filed away somewhere. I'll bet he could tell us the names of some of the other guests who'd be glad to hear the Lodge was open again."

"If we could find the old guest register and create a contact list, then let them know you planned to reopen, it's possible the Lodge could have a full reservation schedule this summer."

"Maybe by midsummer," Zach told her. "I don't know how long it will take the construction crew to repair the roof, gut the damaged rooms and finish renovations."

"Given the layout of the Lodge, I don't think we could partially reopen," she said thoughtfully. "It would be difficult to keep the ongoing construction noise and dust from disturbing the guests."

"I agree." Zach leaned back in his chair, long legs stretched, booted feet crossed at the ankle. "You said 'we'—that sounds as if you've made up your mind to come on board."

She considered him for a moment. "I guess I have." She sipped her coffee, noting the glint of satisfaction in his green eyes. "And you knew I would, didn't you?"

"I hoped you would," he corrected her. "You seemed

like the kind of woman who likes a challenge." He shook his head. "And the Lodge is definitely going to be a test of endurance."

"Oh, I can handle the endurance requirement," she said drily. "I'm just not sure how I'm going to keep my laptop running in all that dust I saw in the office."

He grinned. "We'll set you up in the dining room here at the house until I can get the guys to scrub out the office at the Lodge. I'll move all the file boxes you need from there to here—and the internet connection is good, so you can have access to the web whenever you need it."

"You seem to have thought of everything. Tell me," she said, genuinely curious about his answer, "did it ever occur to you that I might say no?"

"Oh, it occurred to me," he assured her. "But I never planned to accept it. I would have kept showing up on your doorstep until you either took pity on me or got so tired of answering the door that you gave in."

She rolled her eyes, but couldn't help smiling.

By the time she drove back to town two hours later, they'd hammered out a compensation package that included an interim salary sufficient to cover her current expenses, a bonus scale based on the Lodge's growth in income once it opened, and incremental increases in her base salary over the next two years.

Cynthia was satisfied with the deal. Zach had been generous but not a pushover—they'd both made concessions, which was exactly how she liked negotiations to conclude.

As she stepped into the shower to wash away the dust that had inevitably sifted onto her during the tour of the Lodge, she felt good about their agreement and was looking forward to beginning work.

And to seeing more of Zach Coulter on a regular basis.

Cynthia's first day of work began at the Lodge two days later, sorting files into boxes before stacking them along a wall in the office. Finished with the preliminary sorting, she carried the first of the cartons through the lobby, heading outside and away from the interior's dust-filled air. A crew of twenty-plus carpenters, plumbers and electricians swarmed over the building as she reached the porch.

"Here, I'll take that." Zach left a group of men in hard hats studying architectural drawings, and took the box out of her arms. He strode to the back of his pickup, parked across the lot and away from the Lodge, and slid the carton onto the tailgate before shoving it deeper into the truck bed. "Tell me what you want moved and I'll do the heavy lifting," he told her when he'd jogged back to join her on the porch.

"All right," she said mildly.

"You're not going to argue with me?" he asked with amusement as she led the way back into the Lodge and down the hallway to the office area.

"Not when you're offering to move heavy boxes for me," she said over her shoulder as she entered the office. "But give it time, I'm sure we'll have lots of disagreements in the future."

"Thanks for the warning," he said drily. "Which ones do you want in the truck?"

She pointed out the stack of file boxes she'd separated

from the rest of the shambles that was the office, and Zach shouldered one, striding across the room and disappearing through the doorway.

While he was transferring boxes, Cynthia thumbed through the contents of a filing cabinet with the only drawers remaining that she hadn't had time to check.

"You're sure you don't mind working at the house?" he asked her when he returned after carrying off the last box.

"No, not at all." She glanced around at the room. "The dining room table at the ranch house will be much more convenient and I can get started right away. If I stayed here—" she waved at the room "—we'd have to spend a few days cleaning and even then, I wouldn't be able to keep the dirt and sawdust from filtering back in and covering everything. Plus, I'll need to use my laptop and you have internet access at your house."

"All good reasons," he agreed. Hands on hips, he swept the room with an assessing glance. "Anything else you want carried out to the truck?"

"I think that's it." She walked ahead of him out of the office and down the hall to the lobby. "Oh, wait. I wanted to check something." She detoured around the end of the registration counter. The Kiger mustang sculpture no longer hung on the wall behind the counter, but the outline where it had been was clearly visible— the cleaner wood beneath, lighter than the dust-covered wall that surrounded it.

Cynthia quickly opened and closed the drawers below the counter, riffling through the papers inside.

"They're not here," she said, disappointed.

"What's not there?" Zach asked.

"The registration records. I was hoping to find sign-in cards, or lists, or…something." Cynthia rejoined him and they crossed the lobby to step out on the porch.

Zach cupped her elbow to draw her out of the path of a workman pushing a wheelbarrow filled with the metal sconces that had been removed from the lobby's interior.

They zigzagged around a bright yellow dump truck parked beneath second-story windows that stood open. They didn't talk. The noise from workmen tossing discarded furniture, mattresses, fallen ceiling tiles, chunks of plaster and ruined drywall was deafening as the items landed in the bed of the big truck.

Zach walked with her to her car and held the door while she got in. He bent, raising his voice to be heard. "I'll follow you to the house with the boxes."

She nodded, not bothering to reply since she doubted he'd hear her. He closed the door to stride off and Cynthia couldn't resist watching him walk away in her rearview mirror.

She waited until he stepped into his truck before driving away from the Lodge and the hive of activity around it. Trucks were parked along the grassy verge of the lane and she drove slowly, avoiding a battered pickup that had been left jutting out onto the road.

By the time she reached the house and carried her purse and laptop inside, Zach joined her with two file boxes stacked in his arms.

"Where do you want these?" he asked.

"Against the wall is fine," she replied, slipping the strap of her purse over the back of a chair and setting her laptop on the polished cherrywood table. "I feel guilty using this beautiful table for work. What if I spill coffee on it?"

Zach glanced at her and shrugged. "I'm sure it's seen worse over the years." He paused, hands on hips and fingers splayed over his jeans pockets, and studied the table. "Come to think of it, we never used the dining room after Mom was gone. I remember it being piled high with stock magazines and newspapers, but that's about it."

"Maybe that's why it survived so well," Cynthia commented, smoothing her palm over the satiny surface. "It's beautiful."

"That must be due to Mariah. She took care of the house the last few years for Dad."

Cynthia looked around the room with it's long cherrywood table and chairs, the highboy against one wall and the living room visible through the door opposite the entry to the kitchen.

"It's a lovely house. Whoever designed it did a wonderful job."

"My grandfather built it for my grandmother." Zach's gaze followed hers. "When they were newlyweds, he built the cabin down by the creek where Mariah lives. When they were older and he had more money, he had this house built. When Dad and Mom got married, my grandparents moved back into the cabin and insisted my parents move in here."

"So you were born in this house and grew up here?" Cynthia said.

He nodded. "It's kind of funny that Cade's pretty much moved into the cabin with Mariah. I told him that I'd be glad to stay there and they could have the house since there's only one of me. But Mariah's attached to the cabin and wanted to stay there, at least until they get married."

"Will they live in this house after their wedding?" Cynthia asked.

"I expect so—Cade loves raising cattle and running a ranch. The place belongs to all of us and I'm sure he'd like my brothers to stay. But if they do, there's plenty of room to build a house or two."

"What about you? Are you going to stay on the Triple C after you restore the Lodge?" Cynthia said, not sure why his answer was so important to her.

"I never thought I would," he told her. He frowned and his eyes held a shadow. "I have a great job, but since I've been back on the ranch…" He paused before continuing. "I've been reminded just how much I always liked the life of a cattleman. When I leave, I'll miss this place and the day-to-day rhythm of working with Cade here on the Triple C. I've been spending hours in the saddle, moving cattle or riding fence lines and checking for breaks. There's something about being out there, just me and the horse, with all that space around me…" He paused, his gaze flicking to her before his eyes narrowed, his thick lashes concealing his thoughts.

"It sounds like coming home has been good for you," she said gently. Something inside her sang with delight that he wasn't anxious to leave Montana and return to his life in San Francisco.

He nodded, shoulders lifting in a shrug of acceptance.

"So," she said with a smile, "maybe you'll decide to stay and be a cowboy instead of a corporate shark?"

"I don't know." His eyes twinkled, his drawl teasing.

Cynthia knew the moment of stark honesty was gone and he was back to keeping his emotions locked tight. She mourned the loss of the rare glimpse into Zach's deeper feelings.

"I enjoy being a shark, sometimes," he continued. "And my work sends me all over the country, sometimes around the world. I can't imagine giving up a job that's so perfect for me. And there's the added plus that I can choose my own working hours, which means I decide when I want time off and allows me to indulge in my hobbies."

"You mean like climbing really high, very cold, very snowy mountains?" Cynthia teased, smiling at him.

"Yeah, like climbing mountains." His eyes lit, warming as he looked at her. "Or running marathons or surfing the North Shore in Hawaii or..."

"Please don't tell me you ran with the bulls in Italy," she interrupted with a shudder.

"No." He shook his head. "I think those people are crazy. I had enough of being chased by cattle, including a bull or two, when I was a kid on the Triple C. I don't want to run through narrow city streets with a bunch of crazy longhorned bulls breathing down my neck."

"How very wise of you." She was impressed that apparently he was reasonable about not taking some risks. "I'm delighted that what appears to be a suicide wish actually has some sort of limit for you."

"I don't have a death wish," he protested, leaning the point of one shoulder against the doorjamb, his smile slow and teasing. "But I think I was born with a leaning toward pushing the envelope. A thrill-seeker gene, my mom called it."

"So taking risky chances is something you were born to do?" she asked, intrigued by the concept.

He nodded. "Apparently."

Cynthia sighed. "I think I must have been born with a leaning toward caution. What would you call that—a safety-seeker gene?"

His green eyes twinkled, the hard line of his mouth curving upward. "I don't know—I've never heard of a safety-seeker gene."

"Probably because no one wants to admit they have one. 'Thrill seeker' makes a person think of exotic settings and fast cars. What does the term 'safety seeker' bring to mind?" She spread her hands. "I have no idea. See how boring it is? I can't think of a single thing."

Zach laughed out loud.

"See?" she told him. "It not only doesn't sound exciting, it's ridiculous." She pointed at the clock on the wall. "And you need to go away so I can get to work." She made shooing gestures at him and he left, his laughter floating back to reach her ears.

Smiling, she emptied the contents of a box of files onto the table and settled into a chair, quickly becoming engrossed, jotting on her notepad with increasing frequency.

Despite her best efforts, however, thoughts of Zach, his face lit with laughter, kept intruding to distract her.

Chapter Eight

Over the next two weeks, the work on the Lodge moved at a fast pace. Despite a few glitches with late delivery on marble tiles for shower and bathroom walls in the guest rooms, there were fewer problems than Zach had expected. Definitely a surprise and much better than the alternative, he thought.

He wasn't surprised, however, by how much he liked having Cynthia so close. Although her office was technically at the ranch house, she stopped by the Lodge several times a day to check on progress, clarify delivery of items before she paid bills, consult with Zach on final decisions for furnishings and any of a dozen other questions that she needed his input on.

He quickly learned he could rely on her judgment and good taste and would have authorized her to make final decisions on the majority of items. But that would have meant she wouldn't look him up as many times and he liked seeing her. She always made him laugh, and just looking at her gave him pleasure.

And when he walked down the hallway toward the kitchen and dining room after work each night, the faint scent of her perfume teased and lured him.

So far he'd managed to keep their association at work purely business, but he found it increasingly difficult to keep his hands to himself. She was pure temptation, wrapped in a package that was so essentially female that it made his body ache.

He knew, sooner or later, he was going to have to do something about the sexual tension that was a constant hum in the air between them. But they'd settled into such a seamless working partnership that he hated to disturb the rhythm.

Early Friday morning of their second week, Zach rose early. When Cynthia's little red sports car pulled into the ranch yard just before 8:00 a.m., he was waiting on the porch.

He strolled down the sidewalk to meet her.

"Good morning." He held her door while she gathered her purse, lunch and laptop case.

"Hi," she said as she stepped out and he closed the door behind her. "What are you doing here? You're usually down at the Lodge when I arrive."

He took the laptop case from her hand and walked beside her up the sidewalk to the porch. "I have to ride out to check salt blocks and water tanks in the home pastures before I start work this morning."

He pulled open the door and she stepped inside. "Do you ride?"

"Yes, but not very well." She glanced up at him. "Why?"

"I thought you might want to come with me. We both could use a break—the last two weeks have been long days, every day, with no time off."

"I don't know if I should, Zach," she said, walking into the dining room to set her purse on the table. "I have so much to do today. The plumbing distributor needs a decision on the replacement fixtures for the kitchen and I haven't run a cost analysis yet. And—"

Zach halted her speech by laying his index finger over her lips. "I know. There are a million things that have to get done—and they'll all still be here when we get back."

She hesitated, clearly torn.

"You're dressed for riding," he told her, flicking a glance down her jeans-clad legs to the cowboy boots on her small feet. "Except for a hat. We'll borrow one of Mariah's from the tack room in the barn. We'll only be gone a couple of hours," he said. "And if you really need more reasons than that we've worked hard, it's a beautiful morning and we deserve a break, then remember what doctors tell everyone—get away from your desk several times a day and get some exercise. It's good for your physical and mental health."

She laughed and gave in. "All right, you've talked me into it. But I'm really not an experienced rider," she told him as they headed back outside. "So I hope you have a nice, calm horse for me."

"I've already saddled Zelda for you. She's Mariah's mare and she's gentle and smart—even if you tried to fall off, she probably would stop moving and find a way to keep you in the saddle."

"Nice."

Fifteen minutes later, with Cynthia astride Mariah's quiet mare and Zach on Cade's black Andalusian stallion named Jiggs, they left the corrals and rode down the lane that led past the barn and the cabin occupied by Mariah.

The creek ran beside the lane, gurgling and tumbling noisily over the rocky bed on its way to the sandy bottoms and quieter shore near the studio farther away, nearer the Lodge.

"This is a beautiful area," Cynthia commented when they halted so Zach could lean sideways from his saddle and unlatch the gate blocking the lane into the pasture.

"I've always thought so," Zach replied, shoving the gate wide so they could pass through. Once on the other side, he leaned out of his saddle to close and lock the gate securely. He rejoined her and they rode side by side, the lane becoming two parallel dirt tracks as it went farther into the pasture.

"After I've been away, I'm always struck by how quiet it is without the sounds of traffic, sirens and crowds." She waved her free hand, the other holding the reins. "All of the usual urban noise. Which I don't even think about when I'm in the city," she added.

Zach nodded. "You know what always strikes me about being miles away from the city? The night sky. From my condo in San Francisco, I see the city lights for miles, and it's never totally dark. But at 2:00 a.m. here on the ranch, the sky is totally black and hung with stars. Unless the moon is out and even then, I can still see the stars." He tipped his head back and looked up.

The sky was an inverted bowl of deep blue, marked only by a few cottony white, fluffy clouds to the west. The sun was warm on their faces, the air faintly scented with sage.

"I suppose it's fair to say that despite some bad memories, and although I love traveling the world, I've missed Montana and the Triple C," he mused, almost to himself.

"I feel the same," Cynthia commented. "Although for me, it's Nicholas's house in Indian Springs. But even there, I can see the stars at night, which I couldn't do when I was working in the city."

He glanced sideways at her. The brim of the borrowed black Stetson shaded her eyes, but he could see that her mouth curved in a small smile. She sat on the mare with only a touch of awkwardness that Zach suspected would go away with experience. She looked like she belonged here on the ranch, riding beside him on this clear, early summer morning.

The strange sense of rightness in the moment settled deep inside Zach, calming a restlessness he hadn't known existed.

"Why did you choose hotel management?" he asked, curious to know more about her.

"I wanted to travel and I had a friend whose family owned hotels." She glanced at him, mischief lighting her face. "They were Greek, but unfortunately the hotels weren't on the Mediterranean. Most of them were here in the States. During summer breaks, her father wanted her to work in all the different departments of the hotels so she'd be ready to join the family business after graduation. Since I always needed a job, she convinced her father to send me wherever she went. We had a lot of fun—and I discovered I loved working in the hotel industry, and I was also good at it."

"So you're the product of nepotism."

"No," she shot back, bristling. Then she noticed his grin and calmed, smiling briefly. "Are you always going to pull my chain like this?"

"Sounds like a plan to me," he told her mildly. "Especially since you always rise to the bait."

"And that sounds like a fly-fishing term," she told him. "Did you learn that from your dad's fishing buddies?"

"I don't remember. But I know I learned to play poker. Plus, they taught me enough swearwords to get my mouth washed out with soap by my mom."

Her peal of laughter had Jiggs tossing his head, the metal on his headstall chiming.

"I'm sorry," she said when she stopped laughing. "I just had this instant image of you as a six-year-old little boy with a mouthful of soap bubbles."

"It wasn't funny," he told her drily. "And you can't get the taste out of your mouth. I swear, I tasted soap for a week after that."

"Ah, but did you stop swearing?" Her eyes twinkled.

"I stopped swearing where my mother could hear."

Cynthia laughed.

"I bet you never got in trouble when you were a little girl," he said.

"Of course I did," she answered promptly.

"For doing what?" he asked, not convinced.

"Let me think." She pursed her lips, considering. "There was the time I accidentally put my mother's wool sweater in the dryer and it came out so small it fit my doll. And the time we were out of dishwashing detergent so I used the laundry kind and nearly flooded the kitchen with soap suds. Oh, and the worst thing—" she glanced sideways, her blue eyes lit with mirth "—I had a baby chick that died and I wanted to give it a burial, complete with mourners and music. So I put it in a cigar box in the hall closet until I'd planned the funeral. But I forgot it."

"For how long?"

"Too long," she said with emphasis. "My mother kept complaining that the house smelled terrible. The worst part is, she's the one who finally found it." Cynthia's slender shoulders shuddered. "Ugh. It was awful. She sentenced me to early bedtime without supper or TV for a week."

"That sounds a little harsh. How old were you?"

"I think I was six or seven."

"No supper for a week? Even my dad wasn't that tough."

"I was fine—Nicholas waited until her date picked her up in the evening and then he took me downstairs and fed me. I didn't mind giving up TV, so that was no big loss. And Natasha didn't know I read every night before bed, so going to sleep early wasn't a hardship, either." She smiled sunnily.

"All in all, not such a bad punishment for a kid who left a dead chick in the closet?"

"Not bad at all."

"It sounds like your mother dated a lot when you were growing up." Zach wondered if she'd open up and talk about her childhood. From what she'd said, he couldn't imagine her mother being a good parent, but her great-uncle sounded as if he'd been a great substitute.

Cynthia met his gaze, hers direct and clear. "You must have heard at least some of the gossip about my mother before you left Indian Springs. If you're wondering if it's true, then I can tell you that Natasha had an extremely active social life. Still does, for that matter. But I had Nicholas and he was always there." She shrugged. "I consider myself fortunate. He was a great parent, even though he was already in his sixties when I was born."

"Do you have other family? Cousins or aunts, uncles?"

"No. I wish I did. I always wanted to have cousins to play with but my mother was the only child of Nicholas's brother. There may have been other people on my father's side of the family." She looked away, her gaze focused on the old windmill and the water tank below, on the crest of a small hill ahead of them. "Natasha wouldn't tell me who my father is, so I don't have any way to know if I have any relatives there."

She spoke the words with such dignity. Zach felt an urge to protect her, laced with anger at the careless mother who'd left her daughter with so little to hold on to.

"Where's your mother now?" he managed to ask in a level tone. "Does she live in Indian Springs?"

"No." Cynthia shook her head, blond hair shifting against her shoulders. "She hasn't for quite a while. I had a call from her not too long ago…" She paused, frowning. "Actually, she didn't mention where she's living at the moment."

"How do you get in touch with her if you need her?"

Her eyes lit and she smiled, an amused curve of her mouth that mesmerized him. "That doesn't happen. If she needs me, she calls, either my cell phone or the house phone. I don't call her."

"Ah, I see. Somehow, that old saying about letting sleeping dogs lie comes to mind," he said drily.

"Exactly. You're an insightful man, Zach Coulter."

"Thanks, I think." He lifted a hand, pointing at the nearing water tank. "Here's the first windmill."

They rode up to the tank, letting the horses drop their muzzles to the water and drink.

Cynthia tipped her head back, shading her eyes. "I love this old windmill. How long has it been here?"

Zach's gaze followed hers. "As long as I can remember. I'm guessing Granddad might have built it back in the 1930s, maybe."

"There's so much history here on the Triple C," she commented, looking around. "It must be nice to know your family has lived in one place for so long."

"Yeah, I suppose it is." Zach looked at her. "I don't think about it often, but you're right. Maybe that's why I want to pay off the taxes, so Cade and Mariah can raise their kids here."

"They're planning to have children when they get married?" Cynthia's features softened.

Zach shrugged. "That's what they say. I warned

Mariah she might have a kid like Cade, but she said that's okay."

"I think that's lovely, really nice," Cynthia murmured.

"Strangely enough, so do I." Zach knew he sounded surprised. Hell, he thought, he *was* surprised.

"Don't you want to have children some day, a son to teach to ride—or surf the big waves on the North Shore?" she asked.

"No. I can't see myself with kids."

"Why not?" She tipped her head to the side, assessing him. "I bet you'd make a great dad."

"Not a chance. The bad parenting in my family stops with me. Cade's different. He was the oldest and pretty much did what he could for the rest of us after Mom died. He was pretty good at it, and he'll make a great father for some little kid. But the rest of us?" Zach shook his head. "The world's better off if we don't even try."

He tightened the reins, lifting Jiggs's head and walking him around the end of the big tank. The ground immediately surrounding the tank was wet and deeply indented with hoofmarks. Zach reined Jiggs several yards away and uphill from the water to a heavy, thick wooden box. The block of salt inside the box was worn away in scooped indentations from being licked by cattle, but it was still two-thirds its original size. "Looks like everything's okay here. Let's head south to the next tank."

Cynthia and Zelda joined him and they moved on to the next stop on their tour.

By the time they returned to the barn, they'd ridden in a big loop and checked all four of the stock tanks.

"Cade will be glad to hear there aren't any problems with the water," Zach commented as he stepped off Jiggs at the barn. He turned to see Cynthia remove the borrowed cowboy hat and wince as she leaned forward to hook it on a nearby corral post.

He reached her just as she was about to alight and caught her waist, lifting her off the horse. Her hands clutched his shoulders and he lowered her slowly, letting her slide the length of his body until her feet touched the ground.

He nearly groaned aloud at the feel of her soft curves against his and without thinking, he wrapped his arms around her, locking her closer. She didn't protest or push away.

"Thanks." She tilted her head back and looked up at him. "My legs feel like rubber."

"You'll get used to it after we've been riding a few times." He hardly knew what he was saying. He was amazed his brain was functioning enough to form words since all the blood in his body had gone south.

"Are we going riding again?" She sounded delighted, her blue eyes warm.

"Sure." He bent his head, eyes nearly closed as he brushed his lips against her hair. She smelled like fresh air laced with a hint of sage, and beneath that, a flowery shampoo that he thought might be lavender. "Any time you want to," he managed to get out.

"Tomorrow?" Her voice was a murmur of sound, her lips brushing against his throat when she spoke.

"Sure." He lifted his hand and carefully closed his fist over strands of her hair. The pale silk felt like satin against his fingers. He released her hair and brushed the backs of his fingers over her cheek. Her skin was even finer, softer, silkier.

"Zach?" Her voice was faint, breathy. Her fingers clutched the cotton of his shirt.

"Shhhhhh." He replaced his fingertips with his lips, brushing openmouthed, tasting butterfly kisses over the arch of her cheekbone, the tiny beauty mark at the corner of her mouth and at last, the plush softness of her mouth.

He felt her tiny gasp, felt her tense before she went up on tiptoe and slid her arms around his neck. He bent his knees to better align their bodies, and gathered her closer, tighter, as the heat between them grew hotter.

Just when he realized he needed to take her somewhere more private, the sound of an engine broke the quiet morning.

Zach forced himself to lift his head, her lips clinging to his, her blue eyes darkened and dazed.

Behind them, Cade's truck pulled into the yard and parked in front of the house. Zelda's bulk stood between the couple and the house, partially shielding them from view.

Truck doors slammed, and Mariah's laughter drifted across the gravel expanse.

Cynthia's eyes widened, the deep blue no longer hazed but once more sharply aware. She stiffened, stepping back.

"They couldn't see us," Zach said quietly. "Zelda's between us and the house."

Relief flickered across her face. "I'd better go in. I have a lot of work to do today."

He nodded and stepped aside, watching as she walked

away across the gravel yard, her graceful strides quickly carrying her to the house. When she disappeared inside, Zach sighed roughly and turned back to the horses.

He was damned if he was sorry he'd kissed her. He'd been wrong about one thing, though, he thought as he led the horses into the barn to strip them of saddles and tack.

He'd assumed kissing her would ease some of the growing need that had been building with each moment they spent together over the last days.

The pressure hadn't eased. Instead, it was stronger.

It had taken all his willpower to step back and let her walk away when his body was demanding he find the nearest bed and end the torture.

"Hell," he muttered aloud. Despite her wholehearted participation in that kiss, she'd been embarrassed for that brief moment she thought they might have been observed. She had an innocence that he wasn't used to and it brought out a rare, fierce protective streak he didn't know he had. He'd never felt this degree of possessiveness over a woman before.

Frowning, he turned Jiggs and Zelda out into the pasture just behind the barn and drove away from the ranch buildings, down the lane toward the Lodge, determined to bury himself in work and get his mind off Cynthia.

Chapter Nine

Cynthia didn't want to talk about that kiss. When Zach didn't mention it, she breathed a sigh of relief and thankfully picked up their friendly bantering as if it hadn't happened.

Not that she forgot it. In fact, she quickly discovered there was no forgetting it. The memory of his mouth on hers, the taste of his lips, the cool thickness of his hair beneath her fingers, the powerful flex of muscles where her body lay against his—everything about those stolen moments dominated her thoughts when she was alone. In fact, there wasn't a second of her day, whether she was alone or with company, when Zach was far from her thoughts.

Her skin prickled and she had trouble sleeping, tossing restlessly until finally falling asleep. And then she was tortured by dreams that featured Zach.

When Saturday arrived, Cynthia was more than ready

for something to take her mind off the growing attraction between her and Zach.

So when Grady Turner called midafternoon and asked her to join him and his friends at the Black Bear Bar, she immediately said yes.

Just before 9:00 p.m., she left the house and drove the short distance to downtown. A full moon was on the rise in the east and dusk was casting shadows over the street and sidewalks beneath tall maple trees. The heat of the day was fading with the absent sun and she'd wrapped a royal blue silk shawl around her shoulders and throat, leaving one end to trail down her back. Beneath it, she wore a white knit dress trimmed in blue. The narrow blue piping edged the scoop neckline, the hem of cap sleeves and was repeated on the soft tie belt that cinched in at her waist. The skirt was full, perfect for dancing, and she wore her favorite pair of scarlet red heels.

She parked across the street from the Black Bear, ignoring the whistles from a pickup full of teenagers as she crossed the street in the middle of the block. Rock music blared from the radios in the line of cars and pickup trucks slowly snaking their way toward the middle of town and the burger drive-in a block away.

Cynthia smiled, shaking her head at the weekend teenaged ritual before she pulled open the door to the Black Bear and stepped inside.

Grady had been right—the band really was good, she realized with pleased surprise, stretching up on tiptoe to see over the shoulders of a group of cowboys crowding the entry. She didn't see Grady but he'd told her he'd claim a table at the back of the room.

"Excuse me." She tapped on the shoulder of the brawny young man in front of her.

He looked back, saw her and turned, a smile breaking over his face.

"Can I get through, please?"

"Yes, ma'am." He stood back and let her inch past him.

There was just enough room to allow their bodies not to touch and Cynthia was infinitely grateful. After the incident with her mother's boyfriend, who'd grabbed her, kissed her and then groped her when she was twelve, Cynthia had never conquered her instinctive shrinking away from contact with men.

Except with Zach, she realized with shock. She'd never felt the urge to run away from him. In fact, she found herself seeking him out.

She tucked the puzzling truth away to be pulled out and mulled over when she was alone.

She knew the cowboy and his friends watched her as she moved into the crowd, but thankfully none of them tried to stop her. The music was loud, the crowd was noisy and the dance floor was packed, but Cynthia was able to thread her way around the tables between the dancers and the walls without a problem. Still, she was thankful when she located Grady seated at a table several feet away and near the back of the big room.

She lifted her hand and waved, catching his attention.

"Hey," he called, a broad smile breaking over his face. "You made it. Here, take my chair and I'll get another one."

He stood as she neared and held the chair for her.

"Hi, Cynthia." Mariah occupied the next seat with Cade on her far side. The other couple at the table looked familiar and Cynthia realized the woman was also a waitress at the Indian Springs Café, but she didn't recognize the man with her.

"I'm glad you could make it," Mariah continued. "This is my friend Julie and her husband, Bob. Cynthia's a hotel expert. She's working with Zach to get the Lodge ready to reopen."

"Hello." Cynthia smiled. "I think I've met you at the café, Julie."

"Of course." The pretty brunette smiled, her expression open and friendly. "I think I may have waited on you a time or two when you stopped in for lunch. I don't think you've met my hubby, though. Bob is a CPA with an amazing knowledge of tax law, should you ever get in trouble with the IRS."

Bob laughed, his eyes twinkling kindly. "Which I'm sure you're not likely to do. But if you should have any questions about accounting at the Lodge, feel free to call me."

"Thank you, I will." Cynthia relaxed, the easy welcome of Grady's friends soothing any nerves she may have had about her first time back among a social gathering in Indian Springs.

"Glad you could join us, Cynthia," Cade told her.

"Thank you. Grady was pretty insistent." She flicked a quick glance over the crowd. "I'm glad he was. The band is excellent, isn't it?"

Behind her, Grady chatted up a trio of women at a nearby table, leaving them laughing as he returned with an empty chair and promptly sat down. "Bad news—the ladies at the next table told me the band has recently signed a recording contract," Grady put in as he leaned forward and joined the conversation. "Our loss, Nashville's gain."

"Let's hope whoever's booking bands into the Black Bear finds someone as good to take their place," Mariah commented.

"I'll drink to that." Grady lifted his glass and frowned at Cynthia. "Hey, you don't have anything to drink. What do you want? I'm buying."

"A margarita would be great," Cynthia said. The sheer number of bodies in the bar heated the big room and she slipped the shawl off her shoulders, tucking it behind her on the seat.

"You've got it. I'll be right back. You owe me the next dance." He rose and disappeared into the crowd, heading for the long bar against the opposite wall.

"How's everything going with the Lodge?" Cade asked. "Zach's working such long hours I haven't seen him for a few days."

"It's going fine."

The deep male voice directly behind Cynthia sent a shock of heat through her. Afraid her reaction was obvious, she glanced quickly at the other two couples at the table, but they were all focused on Zach.

"Hey, Zach," Cade greeted his brother. "I was wondering if you were going to stop working before midnight and join us."

"Wouldn't miss it." Zach slid into the chair Grady had vacated next to Cynthia, one arm stretched out along the back of her chair. "Grady told me Cynthia was going to be here and she promised the first dance to me."

Cynthia turned her head quickly, her brows forming a faint frown. "When did I promise to dance with you?"

"When we were discussing the paint colors for the two suites at the Lodge."

"We didn't talk about dancing," she said, eyeing him suspiciously. "We talked only about the palettes for the walls and moldings."

"You said the palettes blended and moved well together and I said, you make it sound like they're dancing. Then you said, you supposed that was one way to put it, and I said when are we going dancing, and you said…"

"I said, we're *not*," Cynthia said firmly. "I remember that part very well."

"But then I said, not until we have the chance and a little free time from all the work at the Lodge," Zach finished. His expression was solemn but his eyes twinkled, daring her to laugh with him.

She rolled her eyes as Mariah burst out laughing.

Cynthia looked around and realized the others at the table were watching her and Zach with varying degrees of amazement and amusement.

"What?" she demanded.

"I've never seen Zach get this much opposition from a woman," Cade drawled.

"Probably because they weren't having to argue with him for days on end," Cynthia told him. She looked at Mariah and Julie. "He wanted to paint every wall in the Lodge stark white. And do you know why? Because if it was all the same paint, we could touch it up easily."

"Makes sense to me," Cade said.

"You're *such* a guy," Mariah told him, her affectionate smile taking the sting out of her words.

"I bet it makes sense to Bob, too," Zach said. "Jump in here, Bob, defend me."

"Hey—" Bob leaned back, hands up, palms out "—don't get me involved in this. Julie won't even let me pick out the color of the vegetable we're having for dinner."

"That's because he always picks corn." Julie looked at Cynthia with a what-can-we-do-with-them expression. "I've told him a dozen times that the darker the color of the veggie, the healthier it is for him. But does he listen? Noooooo."

"I like corn," Bob said mildly.

"What are you all arguing about?" Grady rejoined them, sliding a frosted, salt-rimmed cocktail glass across the table in front of Cynthia before snagging an empty chair from another table and sitting down. "Hey, Zach. Glad you could make it."

"I came to dance with Cynthia," Zach told him.

"Yeah?" Grady glanced from him to Cynthia and back again, alert and interested. "Are you dancing with him, babe?"

"Don't call me babe. And, no, I'm not dancing with him." Cynthia licked the salt from the rim of the glass, sipped at the straw and nearly purred. "Thank you for the margarita, Grady." She glanced up through her lashes at Grady before switching to Zach.

"You're welcome," Grady told her. "Why aren't you dancing with Zach?"

"Yeah, Cyn, why aren't you dancing with me?" Zach

asked, his gaze fastened on her mouth pursed around the straw.

"Don't call me Cyn," she replied automatically. "And I'm not dancing with anyone but Grady."

"What?" Zach looked offended and instantly shook his head in denial. "The hell you are."

And before she could protest, he stood, tugged her up out of her chair and towed her behind him onto the dance floor.

"You have *got* to stop manhandling me," she told him, tugging against his hold. "Just because you outweigh me and I'm shorter than you…"

They reached the far side of the dance floor where the corner was darker, far away from their friends, and Zach stopped abruptly, turning her into his arms.

"I'm sorry," he told her, his gaze searching hers. "Do you want me to take you back so you can dance with Grady?"

His voice was sincere. Mollified by his apology, Cynthia shook her head. "No, but I expect you to behave yourself."

"I promise," he said solemnly as he tucked her closer.

"I'm glad you're shorter than me," he murmured in her ear as they moved to the music. "Because you fit just right when I hold you."

She didn't have a comeback. Because he was right. Her head tucked beneath his chin and if he bent his head, his lips would brush against hers just perfectly.

"Remember when I promised I wouldn't make a pass at you when we were working?" he asked her.

She nodded. "Yes, I remember," she murmured.

"We're not working tonight."

She tilted her head back and looked up at him. His face was shadowed in the dim corner but she could easily see the heat in his green eyes and the sensual curve of his mouth.

"I don't think it's a good idea for two people who work together to get involved," she told him, determined to keep her head, although she was tempted. So very tempted.

"I know you don't, Cynthia."

His voice was deeper, rougher, and the way he said the word made it sound as if he meant more by "sin" than just saying her name.

"I'm beginning to think you might believe it's never a good idea for two people to be involved," he told her. "When was the last time you were involved with a guy?"

She considered lying to him, but almost immediately discarded the idea. She wasn't good at lying—one look at her face and he would know.

"Not for a while," she said, not exactly lying but certainly not telling the truth—that she'd never been seriously involved with anyone.

"I'm guessing it didn't end well?"

"I think you could say that." Since the last time she'd had to deal with a man in any situation was her ex-boss and she'd had to quit due to his harassment, she thought that qualified.

"He must have been an idiot."

She smiled, appreciating the dismissive confidence in his words. "I have to say I agree with your assessment," she said with a laugh.

"What?" He pretended to be staggered. "You're actually agreeing with me about something?"

"Oh, stop." Amused, she lightly smacked her palm against the hard muscle of his biceps.

"Yes, ma'am." He pulled her closer, settling his hands at her waist as the band began a slow, dreamy tune.

Cynthia gave in to the seductive sway of their bodies to the music. By the time they returned to the table several songs later, her face was flushed, her pulse racing much too fast.

Zach waited until she sat before bending over her, his hand on her shoulder, his lips brushing the shell of her ear. "I'm going to go to the bar. What can I bring you? Another margarita?"

She nodded and with a brief, intense look, he moved away into the crowd.

Grady shifted into the chair next to her. "You danced with him." His voice held an unspoken question.

"Yes, I did," she confirmed.

"You like him, don't you?"

"Well, of course I like him. He's my boss."

"No, I mean you *like* him," Grady said, speaking slowly.

"Jeez, Grady, this isn't high school," Cynthia said, trying to distract him.

"Don't try to change the subject," he told her. "You let him touch you."

"What?" She stared at him, startled, before collecting herself. "Of course I let him touch me, we were dancing. It's kind of hard to do that without touching."

"You know what I mean," he said with a frown. "He's always touching you, brushing your hair back, resting a hand at your waist." He leaned closer, stared directly into her eyes and said with emphasis, "He's marking you, getting you used to him. This is the courtship dance, Cynthia."

"This isn't courtship," she denied swiftly. "And what do you mean he's marking me? What am I, a horse he's breaking?"

"Protest all you want, Cynthia, but I'm a guy and I know all the signs. He wants you."

"What's wrong with that?"

"Not a thing. Zach's one of the best men I know. I'm just not sure he's the one for you. You could get hurt, Cynthia. He'll be leaving once the Lodge is up and running—and I'm afraid he'll break your heart when he goes."

Grady's blue eyes held a wealth of concern. Cynthia leaned forward and hugged him, pressed an affectionate kiss against his cheek.

"Bless you, Grady. For caring enough to worry about me. I know Zach won't stay in Indian Springs. But he's the first man I've ever felt this way about." She looked at him, willing him to understand. "I'm tired of always being cautious and safe, Grady, I want to take chances. And I want to take them with Zach."

Grady stared at her for a long moment, searching her eyes while worry roiled in his. Then he sighed, patted her arm and sighed loudly once more. "All right. I'd say you've earned the right to kick over the traces and go a little wild. And you couldn't do it with anyone I trust more than I do Zach. But don't fall in love with him," he warned her. "Because if you do and he breaks your heart, I'm gonna have to defend your honor and to tell you the truth." He lowered his voice to a dramatic whisper. "I'm not sure I can take him."

Cynthia laughed, wiped the misty tears from her eyelashes and hugged his shoulders once more.

"Hey, what are you doing with my girl, Grady?"

The two looked up to see Zach nearing the table, several longneck bottles of beer in one hand and a margarita in the other.

Later that night, after several hours of dancing followed by a stop at the restaurant next door with the rest of the group, Zach insisted on following Cynthia home.

She pulled into her driveway and he parked behind her car, walking beside her as they climbed the steps to her porch.

"Why is it so dark out here?" he asked. "Don't you have a porch light?"

"I forgot to turn it on before I left the house tonight," she told him, slipping the key into the lock and twisting. The door moved smoothly inward without a creak, the interior dark and quiet. "Thanks for following me home, Zach," she said, turning to look up at him.

"No problem," he said. The shadows on the porch wrapped them in intimacy. "I'd ask you to invite me in, but I don't think you're ready to say yes." He settled his hands on either side of her waist and gently tugged until her hips snugged against his, her thighs pressed to the long muscles of his. Her hands lifted to settle on his forearms. "Soon, maybe, but not yet," he murmured regretfully. "So I'll settle for a good-night kiss."

He bent his knees, bringing her closer, and covered her mouth with his.

Her fingers tightened on his arms for a moment, but as his lips moved persuasively against hers, she gave in to what they both wanted and slid her arms around his neck, going up on her toes to press her mouth tighter against his.

The fusion of their mouths grew hotter, seconds spinning out. They were both breathless when Zach took his mouth from hers, his hands tightening before he released her. With obvious reluctance, he reached behind her and pushed the door inward.

"I'll see you Monday morning," he told her, his voice gravelly with arousal. "Wear jeans. We'll go riding again."

"All right," she murmured, still dazed from his kiss.

Gently, he moved her across the door sill. He pressed one last swift, hard kiss against her mouth.

"Lock the door," he told her.

She nodded and when he pulled the door shut, she twisted the dead bolt. It wasn't until the lock clicked closed that she heard his footsteps echoing on the wooden porch boards as he left.

She pulled aside the lace curtain on the long, narrow window next to the door to watch as he climbed into his truck and backed out of her driveway. Seconds later, he drove away, the taillights on the pickup winking red as he turned at the end of her block and disappeared.

She didn't realize she was smiling until she was in her bathroom, stripping off her clothes and donning pajamas, and caught a glimpse of herself in the mirror over the vanity.

Her hair was mussed, her eyes glowing and her mouth faintly swollen and bare of lipstick.

Despite her conflicted feelings about Zach and all the reasons she knew she was playing with fire by flirting with him, she couldn't regret anything about the night.

The laughter, fun and excitement of spending the evening with Zach had been exactly what she'd always hoped for when she'd dated other men—and never found.

She'd known he was dangerous the first time she saw him.

She just hadn't realized how much danger he might pose to her own heart.

Chapter Ten

Determined to maintain a professional approach with Zach while at work, Cynthia arrived at the Triple C on Monday to find that the workmen had finished restoring the Lodge office. By 10:00 a.m., all her files and other paraphernalia had been moved out of the dining room at the ranch house and she was settled into her permanent office at the Lodge. Satellite hookups for television and internet had been installed and the kitchen renovation was nearly finished.

With a working bathroom and kitchen, and with the internet connected and functioning, she settled in and was soon immersed in work.

It wasn't until later that afternoon that she realized Zach had moved into the newly completed chef's apartment, located off the back of the kitchen.

"Why are you staying down here instead of up at the house?" she asked as they waited for coffee to brew, leaning against the counter in the kitchen as they talked.

"One of the electricians drove in early this morning and surprised a couple of coyotes near the building supplies stacked on the porch. They ran off when he drove up but I think it's best if I don't leave the Lodge empty at night." He waved a hand at the gleaming professional kitchen. "I've got all the comforts of home with the added benefit of zero commute to work."

"I'm not sure that's such a good thing," she said drily. "If you actually live on-site, when will you ever stop working?"

"Good point." He folded his arms across his chest and shook his head ruefully. "I suppose the honest answer is never."

"Exactly."

The coffeemaker beeped, signaling the end of the brewing cycle, and they filled coffee mugs and left the kitchen. Just before they parted, he brushed his hand lightly over her shoulder and murmured he would see her later. Cynthia turned right down the hallway to her office, Zach turning left to the lobby and she couldn't help remembering Grady's words.

You let him touch you.

Until Grady pointed it out, Cynthia hadn't noticed how often Zach reached out and touched her hair, brushed his fingertips over her shoulder, or rested a hand on her waist when she walked in front of him. She'd never allowed the intimacy with any other male acquaintance. But now that she had with Zach, she found she looked forward to those careful, gentle touches.

Was she letting him slowly but surely seduce her?

Over the next week, Cynthia discovered that working in the same building with Zach was both wonderful and torturous. The weather turned hot, temperatures climbing, and since the air-conditioning wasn't yet functioning in the Lodge, the workers shed T-shirts.

The first time Cynthia walked out of her office and saw Zach shirtless, clad only in boots, jeans and a tool belt, sweat gleaming on his bare chest and arms, she caught her breath and stopped in her tracks. Fortunately, he wasn't looking at her and by the time he turned around, she'd managed to breathe once more and compose her expression. Still, every time she saw him without his shirt, she had to force herself to remember not to stare.

The Lodge was looking better every day. Each morning when Cynthia walked in, she was struck anew by how truly lovely the old building was. Seeing it regain its grace and grandeur was a joy that made reporting for work each day a pleasure, especially when she knew she'd played a key role.

Determined to finish the last ten items on her to-do list, Friday afternoon found Cynthia still at her desk when the construction crew left at six. Absorbed in her work, she had no concept of time slipping by until a rap sounded on the door.

Startled, Cynthia looked up and saw Zach in the doorway. His black hair gleamed, still damp from his shower, and he was dressed in clean jeans, a black T-shirt and boots.

"Are you almost finished? It's after eight o'clock."

Cynthia glanced at her watch and realized he was

right. The two hours since she'd last checked her watch had flown by. "I lost track of time."

"Sign off for the night and come have dinner with me. Mariah dropped off a plate of fried chicken earlier and a bowl of potato salad from the café."

"Yum." Cynthia realized she was starving. "Did she bring dessert from the café?" she asked hopefully.

"Chocolate cake," he said with a grin, "with fudge frosting."

Cynthia nearly groaned. "I'll be right there. I just have to log off."

"Hurry up. If you take too long, I'm eating the cake," he warned.

"No!" she called after him as he disappeared from the doorway. She heard his bootsteps retreating down the hall, followed by muted sounds of activity as cabinets and cupboards opened and closed.

She entered the kitchen several minutes later, after tidying her desk and stopping in the hall bathroom to freshen her lipstick and run a comb through her loose hair.

Silverware and napkins marked place settings at the island and two stemmed glasses sat next to an uncorked bottle of wine. The volume on the radio/CD player installed above a desk tucked into the far corner of the big room was turned down low, and a muted saxophone growled from the local blues station.

Zach turned from the refrigerator just as she walked in. He balanced a foil-covered plate on top of a covered casserole dish in one hand and a large bowl of salad in the opposite palm.

"Let me help you with that." Cynthia hurried to lift

the plate from atop the dish and set it on the counter. "I'll get plates and salad bowls."

They sat side by side on stools at the island counter as they ate.

"I really like this dinnerware we chose," Cynthia commented. "How about you?"

"I like it fine." His lips quirked in a smile. "But it's a stretch to say 'we' as if I had anything to do with it."

"You said you liked this pattern," she protested.

"I asked you which one you liked best, you told me this one, and I said 'me, too,'" he corrected. "And I'm not criticizing, I'm eternally grateful that you have good taste, because trust me," he added earnestly, "I do *not* want to choose china and silverware. Or towels or sheets."

"What about drapes?" she asked, amused by the grimace that followed her question. "I guess not, huh?"

"Definitely not." He picked up the bottle and poured the remaining chenin blanc into their glasses. "I'm happy to help pick the wine, if that helps."

She nodded. "I'll make a note that you've volunteered." Lifting her glass and sipping, she let her gaze move over the room, noting the details. "The kitchen turned out beautifully. I can hardly believe you finished it so quickly. Do you have a guess as to when the rest of the Lodge will be ready?"

"Two weeks, maybe three." His gaze followed hers, assessing the space.

"That's sooner than I thought. I'd better move the search for a chef to the top of my list."

"Do you have any names on the list?" he asked as they finished dinner and dessert.

"A few," she said. "I've been talking to friends at the other hotels where I've worked, then running background and reference checks on the people they've recommended. Some of them sound interesting, but I haven't set up interviews yet. I also thought it might be good to search in the surrounding counties here in Montana."

He nodded his approval, his wineglass cradled in one hand. "Sounds good to me. I like employing locals if possible. Have you found any candidates closer to home?"

"The owner of the Indian Springs Café highly recommended a woman named Jane Howard. Evidently she grew up on a ranch in the area, but was gone for several years, then returned and has worked her way up through the ranks to assistant chef at the Black Bear Restaurant in Indian Springs."

"Why don't we check her out this weekend? I'll pick you up tomorrow at seven and we'll have dinner at the Black Bear, then catch a movie."

And just that quickly, the easy interchange between them shifted, suddenly charged with sexual tension that thickened the air until Cynthia could barely breathe.

She'd thought about this, about how she would answer if he asked her to go out with him. She reminded herself that a date was just a part of the courtship dance Grady had alluded to—not a promise she would end the evening in bed with him.

"I'd like that," she murmured, her voice husky.

His eyes flared, widened before they narrowed, the gleam of satisfaction clearly readable along with heat.

"Good." He leaned forward, brushing a kiss against her mouth. "It'll be fun."

"Yes," she told him when his lips left hers. She slid off her stool, gathered up dishes and walked across the black-and-white tile to the sink. "We can check out Jane Howard's cooking at the same time we're checking out the competition in the Black Bear."

"I was thinking more along the lines of enjoying each other's company," he drawled, collecting the rest of the dirty china and joining her. He set the plates on the counter next to the sink and slid his arms around her waist, her back against his chest, and bent to press a kiss against the sensitive skin beneath her ear. "Much as I admire your devotion to your job, I'd like to forget it for one night."

"Do you think we can?" She turned her head to meet his gaze, their faces barely inches apart.

"Yeah," he said with slow certainty. "I'm sure we can."

He turned her to face him, one hand tangling in her hair to gently tug her head back, turning her face up to his before he kissed her.

Cynthia wrapped her arms around him and kissed him back, willingly following where he led, totally absorbed and lost in the sheer pleasure of his mouth on hers, his hard body wrapped around hers. He was seducing her every time he kissed her. She knew it. She couldn't bring herself to care.

The phone rang, the sound breaking the taut quiet, then rang again.

Zach lifted his head with a frustrated growl and stretched over the counter to reach the portable phone he'd set there earlier. He glanced at the caller ID and thumbed the speaker button.

"Hey, Cade, what's up?" Zach nuzzled the tender skin beneath Cynthia's ear. She shivered and tilted her head to the side to allow him better access.

"We've found Brodie." Cade's deep voice sounded loud in the quiet room.

Zach froze, his lips pressed against the vulnerable curve of Cynthia's soft throat, his arms tightening around her. Then he lifted his head.

"Where?"

"He's in a rehab unit in Ukiah, California. The detective used the information Angela found and visited him there. Whoever checked Brodie in used the wrong name on the hospital records—they have him listed as J. C. Brodie."

"Is he all right?" Zach's muscles were tight, tensed against hers.

Cynthia held her breath, praying Zach's younger brother wasn't badly hurt.

"The detective says he was thrown by a bull at a rodeo held at a ranch near Ukiah. There was already unhealed damage from a prior injury—I'm guessing from the fall he took in New Mexico earlier. His right leg is in traction."

"How bad is it?"

"I don't know. The detective asked, but Brodie wouldn't give him any details. He told him to pass the word to us that he's okay, but he'll be laid up for a while and he doesn't know when he'll be able to get back here. The detective said Brodie wanted him to tell us he'll call."

"Huh." Zach was silent, tension coming off him in waves.

Cynthia slid her fingers through the thick hair at his nape in an unconscious effort to soothe.

"I don't believe him," Zach said after a moment. "Something's wrong. My gut's telling me we should get on a plane and fly to California."

"I thought you'd say that. My gut's telling me the same thing. I'm hanging up and phoning the airline. I'll call you back with the flight times."

"I'll pack my bag."

The click as Cade cut the connection was audible over the speaker phone and Zach stretched once more to switch off the receiver.

"You have to go," Cynthia said softly. She tipped her head back to search his face. To anyone else, she knew his expression might seem smooth and calm, but she'd come to know him over the past few weeks. She clearly read the worry in his darkened green eyes, the small, almost unnoticeable flex of a muscle along his jawline, the faint tightening of the line of his mouth.

"Yeah, I have to go." He cupped her face in his palm and pulled her closer. From thigh, waist, breast to chest, they were pressed together, the heat pouring off his much bigger body, warming her. He bent to brush kisses over the curve of her cheek, the arch of her cheekbone and brow, the sensitive corner of her mouth. "Remember where we left off," he said. "When I get back, I want to pick up exactly where we stopped." And his mouth took hers, the kiss holding frustration beneath a promise of pleasure and seduction.

When at last he lifted his head, they were both

breathing faster and Cynthia echoed his obvious reluctance when he drew her arms from his neck and stepped back.

An hour later, he was gone, heading for the Turner ranch with Cade, where Grady would use his Cessna to fly them to the airport in Billings. From there, they would catch a commercial flight to California.

With Zach gone, Cynthia thought the Lodge seemed curiously empty, the energy muted in the big building despite the continued sound of carpenters hammering and delivery trucks coming and going.

On Monday, she drove downtown to run errands before heading to the Triple C for the day. She stopped at the library to collect an armload of cookbooks she wanted to skim before beginning her search for a chef to run the Lodge's kitchen. She had several more stops on her list, each of which took longer than she'd intended. When she glanced at her watch, she realized it was nearly noon and with quick decision, she parked down the block from the Indian Springs Café and stepped onto the sidewalk.

The café was a beehive of busy waitresses and diners when she pushed through the doors. Fortunately for Cynthia, Mariah was working.

"I have one empty booth in the back," Mariah told her with a welcoming smile. "Come with me."

"Thanks." Cynthia followed her as she moved with easy familiarity around the tables to reach the far corner of the long room.

"Here you go." Mariah handed her a menu as she slid onto the bench seat. "One of us will bring you water in a sec—do you want anything else to drink? Coffee, iced tea?"

"Iced tea would be lovely," Cynthia said gratefully.

"You got it. It's crazy busy in here, but I'll be back to take your order in a few minutes."

She bustled off to collect loaded plates from the kitchen pass-through window behind the long counter.

Cynthia set her purse beside her on the blue upholstered bench and opened the menu. It only took a moment to decide on the soup with salad special and she closed the vinyl-covered folder just as Mariah returned with a glass of iced tea and a long straw.

"Know what you want?" Mariah asked, whipping out a pad and pen.

Cynthia told her and with an apology for not staying to chat, Mariah hurried off to take an order from another customer.

While Cynthia waited for her salad and soup to arrive, she took a notebook from her purse and jotted notes for meetings with plumbers and masonry contractors scheduled after lunch in the workday ahead. Although they'd accomplished far more at the Lodge than she would ever have thought possible in the beginning, there was still so much more to be done before they could book guests.

"Good morning."

Cynthia glanced up. A man stood next to her booth. He was dressed in dark slacks and a cream-colored dress shirt open at the throat beneath a light brown sports jacket. His brown hair was cut short with a neat side part, his smile affable and confident.

Something about him seemed very familiar, but for the life of her Cynthia couldn't place him.

"Good morning." She returned his smile with polite reserve. He wouldn't be the first strange man to approach her in a public place and unfortunately, she thought with a sigh, he no doubt wouldn't be the last.

"I don't know if you remember me, Cynthia," he continued, his smile never faltering. "We went to school together. I'm Jim Meyers."

"Of course." She did remember him, she realized, but not fondly. She scanned the neat hair, brown eyes, smooth confidence oozing from every pore, and decided he hadn't changed all that much except to grow older. He'd been the spoiled only child of a local land developer and she'd never liked him. "How are you, Jim?"

"I'm well. May I?" Without waiting for her permission, he slid onto the bench opposite her and fixed her with a friendly smile. "And you?"

"I'm well." Cynthia smiled faintly, her pen poised above her notebook, waiting for him to explain why he'd approached her.

"Excellent." He beamed at her. "I understand you've taken on the management position out at the Coulter Lodge."

"That's right." She nodded, a small dip of her head.

"I was surprised to hear Zach Coulter had returned to renovate the place." He shook his head, his expression concerned.

"Why is that?" She asked with a slight lift of one eyebrow.

"Well, we all know Zach has gone on to bigger and brighter city lights than our nice small town," he said.

"It's unlikely he'll stay involved with the Lodge and once he loses interest, it will return to its former state. A shame really," he said dolefully, his eyes sharp as he studied her face.

"I didn't realize you and Zach knew each other so well," Cynthia commented mildly, wondering what motive he had for the conversation. He clearly had an agenda and was leading up to something with his comments, but she wasn't sure what that might be.

"I wouldn't say we're best friends," he said with a smile. "I was a few years behind him in school and as you know, he left Indian Springs as soon as he could. No, my conclusions are based on generally held opinion in Indian Springs—and facts, of course."

"And what facts are those, exactly?" Cynthia asked, pretending to be objective, though inside she was seething. His comments might seem innocent enough on the surface, but his inflection subtly inferred Zach had no ability to commit to the Lodge project and no staying power, long-term. She didn't believe the majority of Indian Springs residents thought Zach was unprincipled and undisciplined. She couldn't help but wonder why Jim was trying so hard to convince her the town had so little respect for Zach.

"Why, that the Coulter brothers shook the dust of Indian Springs from their boots more than a decade ago and only returned to collect their inheritance, of course."

"Really?" Cynthia sipped her tea.

"I've heard Zach inherited the Lodge and the surrounding acres it sits on. I'm sure he'll be selling it and heading back to San Francisco after the opening."

Ah, Cynthia thought. *So that's where this conversation is going.* "Do you think so?" she said aloud, widening her eyes as if surprised by his revelation.

"Of course." He shrugged. "It's probably for the best, since it's unlikely Zach will stay in Indian Springs and businesses always do best when the owner stays involved. The best guarantee of a failed business is an absentee owner," he added with conviction.

"I suppose that's true," Cynthia said noncommittally.

"Studies prove it's true," he told her. "I hope he sells to someone local, someone involved in our community with plans to stay in the area." He paused, eyeing her expectantly.

"That certainly sounds as if it would be best," she agreed.

He lowered his voice and leaned closer. "I'd be interested, should he decide to sell."

"Would you?" She managed to force a note of approval into her own voice though she was having difficulty being polite.

"Yes, I would." He nodded, a brief, visible confirmation of his good intentions. "In fact—" he paused, as if the thought had just occurred to him "—you could be a big help to the community, Cynthia."

"How is that?" she asked, feigning interest.

"If you would agree to intercede and arrange a meeting with Zach for me, I'd like to make him an offer to buy the Lodge, the cabins behind it and the land they sit on, including the water frontage on the creek bank. For the good of the community, of course," he added hastily.

Cynthia guessed her expression must have reflected her distaste for his request. "How would it be good for the community if you owned the Lodge?" she asked, struggling to maintain a cool, politely interested façade.

He spread his hands, the affable smile back on his face. "I'm a local boy. Always have been—always will be. I don't have aspirations to travel to the big city and set the world on fire. My roots are sunk well and truly deep here in Indian Springs."

"But you've never been an innkeeper before," she pointed out. "In fact, your family has spent several generations buying up land and developing it, often to the detriment of the neighbors. Why would I think you would keep the Lodge intact and not break the land into pieces and sell it off?"

"I assure you, Cynthia," he began.

"Not to mention—" she broke in "—that the only access to the Lodge is across Coulter land. How on earth do you think you would have access to it for ingress and egress? Do you actually think the Coulters would let you open up their ranch to strangers driving across it?"

"All of that would have to be negotiated, of course." His smile was no longer as friendly. "But nonetheless, I'd like to talk to Zach about the proposition. He hasn't returned my calls. I'd appreciate your facilitating contact with him. In fact, I'm willing to make it worth your while."

Before Cynthia could reply, Mariah interrupted them.

"Here's your lunch, Cynthia." She slid a plate on the tabletop in front of Cynthia.

"Thanks, Mariah." Cynthia looked up and into Mariah's brown eyes.

"No problem—enjoy." Mariah cast a troubled glance at the man sitting across from Cynthia before she turned and hurried off.

Cynthia leveled a chilly stare at him. "It's not my job to arrange appointments for Zach. If he wants to speak with you, he can make that decision without my assistance. If you can't reach him by phone, I suggest you send him a letter with any requests."

"Very well." Jim Meyers rose, pausing to look down at her, his brown eyes hard. "Don't make the mistake of choosing the wrong side in this, Cynthia."

"I don't have a side. I work for Zach Coulter. Therefore, my loyalties are to him. And now that we've cleared that up, I believe our conversation is done."

He narrowed his eyes at her, muttered an oath under his breath and turned to stride out of the café, his movements conveying the depth of his irritation.

Cynthia drew a deep breath and counted to ten.

Jim Meyers had been obnoxious as a kid and apparently he hadn't grown better with time. If anything, she thought, he was worse.

She picked up her spoon and tasted the soup, determined to forget the unpleasant incident as soon as she'd told Zach about it. But she had the uneasy feeling Jim Meyers wasn't going to go away soon, and that his interest in the Lodge meant potential trouble for Zach.

Chapter Eleven

The Ukiah Memorial Hospital sat on the crest of a hill, the backside of the building looking out on the Northern California redwoods. The front of the building was modern brick and faced the large parking lot where the hot sun heated the asphalt pavement, bouncing off the black surface in visible waves to assault the eyes.

Zach and Cade parked their rental car in the lot and entered the building. After a brief stop at the information desk, they rode the elevator to the second floor and strode down a hallway that smelled of antiseptic.

They heard Brodie before they saw him.

"Hell, no, I'm not eating this. I need real food—doesn't the kitchen know how to grill a steak?"

Zach felt a swell of relief. Brodie's irritated roar sounded normal.

He and Cade stepped into the room and paused. Their brother was in bed, his right leg propped up on pillows. Beard stubble darkened his jaw, his black hair was mussed and longer than it'd been the last time they'd seen him, and his green eyes glowed with irritation.

The middle-aged nurse standing at his bedside merely smiled at him. "Sorry, Mr. Coulter, but the kitchen is on a budget. No steaks."

Brodie fumed. Zach could almost see the steam coming from his ears.

"Damn, Brodie," he said mildly. "Give the lady a break. You can't expect steak and lobster lunches in a hospital."

Brodie's head snapped around, his eyes narrowing over Zach before flicking to Cade. His frown eased, replaced by a wide grin.

"Zach, what are you doing here? Hey, Cade."

Zach reached the bed and caught his brother's hand in a tight clasp. "You look like hell, bro," he said bluntly.

"Thanks, Zach." Brodie grinned as Zach stepped back and Cade greeted him with the same handshake.

"Ignore him, Brodie," Cade said easily. "That's what I told him when he showed up at the Triple C after climbing a mountain—he's just passing it on."

Zach and Cade pulled up a pair of plastic metal-legged chairs and sat, their long legs stretched out in front of them.

"So what brings you two to California?" Brodie asked. "I told the detective I'd call as soon as I knew when the doc was ready to let me out of here."

"We wanted to see for ourselves just how bad your leg was damaged," Zach said bluntly. "You have a history of telling us you're fine when the doctors are going ballistic."

"Yeah," Cade added. "So, what's the real story?"

"I broke my leg in two places." Brodie's face was somber. "I'm done with bull riding. No more rodeos."

"Damn, I'm sorry." Zach couldn't imagine his brother not riding bulls and following the rodeo. He'd been doing it since he was barely a teenager—it was his life. That Brodie wouldn't be riding bulls anymore was as inconceivable as it would be if he himself stopped climbing mountains or never again tried breaking another record. "Have any idea how long before you're released from here?"

"No." Brodie scrubbed his hand down his face. He raked the thick strands of his hair back from his forehead. "But I go from here to a rehab center across town. How long I have to stay there depends on how fast I can learn to walk again."

Zach didn't want to ask if Brodie would eventually walk unaided or if he'd need a cane. "What can we do?"

"Nothing. I hate the waiting, but the doc says if I don't stay off my leg and let the bone heal, I'll be here longer. And I'm already damned sick of this place." He waved a hand. "Don't get me wrong. The nurses are nice and the doctors are great, but this is the last place I want to lie around."

"What happened?" Cade asked, his deep voice quiet.

"I climbed aboard a rank bull in a friend's corral and he threw me into the fence." Brodie's words were blunt. "I might have been okay but I'd damaged the leg a few months earlier in New Mexico. It wasn't entirely healed."

"Maybe you're getting too old to ride crazy bulls," Zach drawled. He knew Brodie well—if either he or Cade got sentimental, Brodie would close up like a clam. He'd never wanted anyone worrying over the scrapes, bruises and broken bones he'd earned on his way up the ladder to rodeo champion.

"Yeah, right." Brodie snorted. "Like you're too old to do whatever crazy thing you've been doing. What is the most recent thing, by the way?"

"Mount Everest," Cade put in. "He climbed Mount Everest."

"Damn, Zach," Brodie said, clearly impressed. "That's pretty cool."

"It was." Zach nodded in agreement. "And cold. Very cold."

Masculine laughter filled the room. Out in the hallway, the nurses on duty glanced significantly at each other and breathed sighs of relief. The handsome patient in room 205 hadn't laughed since he was admitted.

"The detective told me Dad was gone," Brodie said, all laughter gone as he eyed them with somber determination. "But he didn't say why you two are back in Indian Springs."

"Dad left the Triple C to the four of us," Zach told him. "Evenly split four ways."

"That's not possible," Brodie said flatly. "Why would he do that? He hated our guts."

Zach shrugged. "That's what I thought, but Cade's fiancée says otherwise."

Brodie's head snapped around and he stared at Cade. "Fiancée? You're getting married?"

Cade smiled. "Yeah. Her name is Mariah Jones. She

lived on the Triple C the last few years. She took care of Dad after he was diagnosed with lung cancer."

It was difficult for Zach to tell whether Brodie was more stunned by Cade being engaged, their father leaving them the Triple C, or the news that Joseph Coulter had let a stranger live on the ranch.

"Speechless, aren't you?" Zach drawled, grinning when Brodie lifted his hand and made a rude gesture. "Lots of things have changed in Indian Springs, Brodie. I'm renovating the Lodge and plan to open it within a few weeks. Cade's getting married and she's not only pretty, she's nice—which is why I still haven't figured out how he talked her into saying yes. Oh, yeah," he added, "Dad not only left us four the ranch, he left individual assets to each of us. You get the horses."

Brodie went still. "What horses? Are the Kigers still there?"

"We don't know," Cade told him. "When you come home, we'll go looking. From what Mariah and the two ranch hands tell me, no one's been out to Tunk Mountain for years." He shrugged. "Maybe you'll get lucky."

"I'll be damned." Brodie looked stunned. "I thought the old man sold them off."

"I can't find any record of them being sold and I've gone through all the files in Dad's office," Cade told him. "If I knew for sure the horses were there, I'd ask you to let us round them up and sell them. The inheritance tax on the Triple C is huge and Dad was broke when he died."

Brodie frowned. "That doesn't make sense."

"He'd stopped working the ranch except for planting alfalfa in the flats and running Hereford cattle in the home pasture," Zach told him. "From what the neighbors and the Turner brothers told us, Dad cut himself off from nearly everyone he knew and barely kept the ranch out of debt."

"Did he leave a lot of bills?" Brodie asked, his gaze landing on Zach.

Zach shook his head. "No. The only debt is Uncle Sam and the inheritance tax—and that's huge."

"How huge?"

"Two million dollars, give or take a few thousand."

Brodie whistled, a long, slow sound.

"That's a lot of money," he said.

"If we sell off enough land to pay the taxes, the ranch will be too small to build a profitable business," Cade told him.

"Cade sold cattle, I'm going to run the Lodge. If we agree to keep the Triple C, we'll all have to be creative in raising money to clear the tax debt." Zach shifted in the too-small and uncomfortable chair, crossing his ankles and watching Brodie's face from beneath the brim of his Stetson.

"If I had that much cash, you could have it. But I don't," Brodie said. "And I'm not going to be much use to you for the next few months, not with this leg." He brooded as he stared at his swollen, blackened toes visible at the end of the leg cast. "I don't give a damn about the ranch. I swore when I left that I'd never go back and I still don't want to. I'll sign over my share to you two and you can do what you want with it."

Zach glanced sideways at Cade, who lifted an eyebrow slightly.

"Well, if you were serious about handing me a quarter

of a ranch that's potentially worth millions of dollars, I'd take it," Zach drawled. "But even if you were willing to give it up, we couldn't legally accept it. The will specifically says it's all or none. If we're all willing to sell the place, we can. If we don't all agree, it can't be done."

"Hell." Brodie looked disgusted. "Leave it to the old man to make life difficult, even from the grave."

"Why don't you think about it, Brodie?" Zach told him. "By the time you're out of rehab, maybe you'll change your mind."

"Not likely. I don't want to go back to the Triple C—there's nothing there but bad memories and I don't want to revisit them."

"Tell you what, Brodie." Zach bent his knees and sat forward, leaning his forearms on his thighs. "If you feel the same way when you check out of rehab, all you have to do is come back to the Triple C for Cade's wedding. By then, if you still want to, I'll find a way around the will so you can walk away from the ranch and never have to see it again."

Brodie stared at him, dark brows lowering, his green gaze brooding. "All right," he said at last. "Deal."

"Great." Zach slapped his hands on his knees and stood up. "Now I'm going to go find a steak house and bring back three New York steaks, medium rare, with all the trimmings. What else do you guys want?"

"Bring me two steaks," Brodie said, looking at his tray of hospital food with distaste. "I feel like I could eat a whole damn cow."

Cynthia walked out of the Lodge office in bare feet, heading for the kitchen. Only the light over the island was lit and the soft light gleamed over the kitchen's new countertops and stainless steel fittings.

Making a mental note to move the search for sous chefs and waiters to the top of her to-do list, she padded silently across the black-and-white tiled floor and found a container of yogurt from her lunch in the restaurant-sized refrigerator. Locating a spoon in the utensil drawer, she tossed the foil lid in the trash can and ate the strawberry yogurt while leaning against the sink. The big window gave her a view of the pastures that stretched to reach the rise of flat-topped buttes in the distance, the moon highlighting their tops and casting shadows down their sides and out across the prairie.

It's beautiful here, she thought. *No wonder the Lodge was once packed with guests.*

Vowing that it would be again, Cynthia washed her spoon and returned it to the drawer, tossed her empty yogurt container in the recycling bin and left the kitchen.

Just as she was crossing the lobby to return to the office, the front door opened.

Before she could do more than gasp in surprise, Zach stepped inside.

"Zach!" She pressed her one hand over her racing heartbeat. "You startled me— I didn't know you were coming home tonight."

"Sorry, I didn't mean to scare you." He dropped his duffel bag at the foot of the stairs and walked toward her. "What are you doing here so late? It's after ten. You're not still working, are you?"

"I had a few things I wanted to finish before I left tonight. The moving crew is delivering the rest of the lobby furniture and some of the bedroom furnishings tomorrow and I wanted to make sure everything was ready for them."

"I wish you wouldn't work so late, but nonetheless…" He stopped with the toes of his boots nearly touching her bare feet and slipped his arms around her waist. "I'm glad you're here," he murmured as he bent his head, his lips brushing the corners of her mouth before settling fully against hers.

It felt so natural and right to be wrapped in his arms, his mouth on hers, to welcome him home. On some level, Cynthia registered that it was dangerous to be growing so accustomed to being in his arms and his life. When he left, he was going to break her heart. But she ignored the faint warning, giving in to the sheer pleasure.

When he lifted his head, he didn't release her. Instead he tucked her closer and pressed his cheek on the top of her head where it rested against his shoulder.

"Did you see Brodie?" she asked, her palm against his chest, fingers toying with a smooth mother-of-pearl button on his shirt.

"Yeah, we saw him."

Caught by the somber note in his voice, Cynthia tilted her head back and looked up at him. "What's wrong?"

He sighed, his eyes dark. "He's finished riding rodeo bulls."

"Oh, I'm so sorry, Zach. He was at the top of his field, wasn't he." It wasn't a question.

"Yeah—and it took him years to get there." He shook

his head. "I can't imagine Brodie without rodeo. It's all he's ever wanted since he was five years old."

"Is there something else he can do that will let him stay involved in rodeo?"

"There might be, although I don't know what it could be. Even if there were something, I can't see Brodie settling for watching from the sidelines. And who knows if he'd even be able to do that."

Zach's voice held grim worry.

"Are you saying he might not recover from this?" Cynthia was shocked.

"It's possible. Cade and I talked to his doctor before we left the hospital. There's still a possibility Brodie might lose the leg. And even if all goes well, they don't know if he'll recover fully. It's likely he may have to walk with a cane for the rest of his life."

"How does Brodie feel about that—did he tell you?"

"He says he's going to walk." A small smile flitted over Zach's face. "Knowing how stubborn he is, I'm putting my money on Brodie."

"Good." Relieved by that small lightening of Zach's worried face, Cynthia hugged him tighter. "I'm glad. So, when are you expecting him back at the Triple C?"

"I'm not sure he'll ever come back."

"What?" Cynthia leaned back to stare up at him. "Why not?"

"He told us that he swore he'd never come back when we all left thirteen years ago. Even though Dad's gone now, Brodie says there are too many bad memories here and he doesn't want to revisit any of them. We tried everything we knew to convince him, but when Cade and

I got on the plane to leave California and come home, neither of us were convinced he'll be back."

"But what about the Triple C? I thought you all had to join forces if you're going to have any chance to save it?"

"That's our only ace in the hole," he told her. "I don't think Brodie will let the rest of us down when we need him. And if we can get him back on the Triple C, I think he'll stay. He and Cade always loved this place, maybe more than Eli and me. With Cade, it's the land and the cattle. With Brodie, it's the land and the horses."

"And your father left him the horses and a piece of the land," Cynthia said softly. "I think maybe your father knew you better than any of you realized."

"Maybe he did," Zach said with skepticism. "But if so, he had a hell of a way of showing it. He blamed us for mom's death. I don't remember a kind word from him after Mom died."

"Why did he leave you the Lodge and a quarter of the Triple C?" she asked, curious.

"If we're going to go with your assumption that Dad knew all of us better than we ever realized, then the land's a no-brainer. Like my brothers, I grew up here and my sweat and a few pints of my blood is in the ground of the Triple C. And the Lodge…" He paused, his eyes losing focus as if he were thinking of something Cynthia couldn't see. "Maybe because restoring it is a challenge and a risk—and everyone knows I was born with a competitive streak a mile wide." His gaze sharpened, his mouth curving in a smile that held cynicism. "But to buy your theory, we'd have to believe that

Joseph Coulter gave a damn about his sons and I'm here to tell you, honey, he didn't."

Cynthia searched his face, looking for any hint that Zach cared if his father had regretted his treatment of his sons, but found no indication. Still, she sensed a deeper emotion beneath the cynicism. She decided to let it go, for now.

"You must be tired after your trip. Did you have dinner?"

"Cade grabbed a burger on the way out of Billings but I wasn't hungry— I am now, though. Anything good in the refrigerator?"

She nodded. "I cut up a salad earlier and Mariah dropped off groceries for you in case you came home tomorrow. We didn't expect you tonight, but she said she was putting a package of steaks in the meat drawer."

"Come on." He released her, his hand sliding down her arm to catch her hand, his fingers threading through hers. "Keep me company while I eat."

Cynthia went without protest. It was astounding how comfortable she felt with him, she thought as they worked together in the kitchen.

Was it possible there could be more between them than the undeniable sexual attraction that she knew simmered constantly below the surface?

And more important, if there was a chance for a deeper connection for her with Zach, was she brave enough to step outside her safe, solitary world and trust him?

Chapter Twelve

It wasn't until later, as they sat on tall stools at the island counter, and all that remained of Zach's dinner were a few crumbs and a small steak bone, that Cynthia paused, lowering her glass of wine to the tile countertop.

"I just realized—I totally forgot to ask if Brodie knew how to reach Eli."

"He doesn't, but he's pretty sure Eli's in Spain."

Cynthia blinked. "Spain?"

"Brodie visited him in Santa Fe several months ago. Eli told him he was thinking about taking an internship with a master silversmith in Spain. But if Eli mentioned the name of the silversmith or what town in Spain, Brodie doesn't remember."

"But at least you have a bit more information and a place to start looking. If Eli left the States, that would certainly explain why the detectives have been frustrated with dead ends after following every lead."

"We reached the same conclusion," Zach agreed. "But we have no idea where to start."

"I wonder if you could search for Spanish silversmiths on the internet?" Cynthia asked.

He nodded. "I thought of that. I emailed Angela and asked her to begin looking. If he's surfaced in any news reports, she'll find it."

"Does he belong to any artisans' organizations here in the States? If so, maybe he's renewed his registration with a current address."

"We've already tried that," Zach told her. "He renewed more than one, but each time he used the address of the P.O. Box in Santa Fe—the same mail stop he's had for the past ten years."

Cynthia thought a moment, lips pursing as she considered and discarded several potential ways to unravel the trail that would eventually lead to Eli. At last, she shook her head. "I give up. This is worse than trying to solve a Rubik's cube."

He laughed and leaned closer to top up her wine from the nearly empty bottle they shared. "So you're not big on puzzle solving?"

"I like crossword puzzles," she told him. "And I also like guessing who committed the murder on *CSI* every week. I'm pretty good at those two, actually, but sadly, not so good with the Rubik's Cube."

He propped his elbow on the countertop, his chin on his hand, their knees bumping as they faced each other on the tall stools. "You constantly surprise me, Cyn."

"Why is that?" She sipped her wine, savoring the fruity taste.

"Because you don't care whether it matters to anyone

if you can solve a puzzle. You are who you are. People can take it or leave it."

"Some people would say that's not a good thing," she commented.

"Some people are fools," he said simply. "While you're clearly a very smart woman."

She searched his face and found only sincerity. "Thank you," she murmured.

"For what?"

"For seeing who I am. For telling me it's okay. For not assuming the sum total of who I am begins and ends with the size of my breasts and the color of my hair."

"You're welcome." He leaned forward and brushed a soft kiss against the sensitive skin at the corner of her mouth. "Don't get me wrong," he said, his deep voice a murmur in the quiet room. "I love the size of your breasts and the color of your hair." He smoothed a strand of her hair between his thumb and forefinger, then tucked it behind her ear, his hand stroking over her shoulder and down her arm until his fingers threaded through hers. He laid her hand on his thigh, palm down and just above his knee before he covered it with the warmth of his much larger hand. "But you're much more than that."

Cynthia didn't know what to say. "I…" Her throat closed and she paused. "I wish I'd known you when I was younger, before…things happened."

"I wish I'd known you when you were younger, too," he said softly. "What things happened? Can you tell me?"

She searched his eyes and found only warmth. "It's a common enough story. And I'm not the only girl in

America whose mother had boyfriends that were too friendly with her daughter." Beneath her palm, she felt the muscles of his thigh flex and tighten but his expression didn't change. Reassured, she continued, "I was luckier than lots of other girls, because I wasn't raped."

"But someone scared you," he guessed, green eyes darkening.

She nodded. "When I was twelve, my mother was dating an older man. He seemed to have plenty of money to buy her gifts and take her to nice places. But he drank a lot and Nicholas didn't like him—neither did I. One day the man came to the house looking for my mother. I told him Natasha wasn't home but he pushed his way inside and said he'd wait. Nicholas came home from the grocery store just in time to pull him off me."

Zach growled, a low, rumbling sound. Startled, Cynthia stopped speaking.

"Sorry, honey." He lifted her hand from his thigh, his lips warm where he pressed a kiss into her palm before lowering it once more. "I wish I'd been there. I hope Nicholas did some damage when he threw him out."

"I remember a lot of yelling. Natasha was furious with Nicholas later because she said he'd blackened the man's eye, but Nicholas always swore he never hit him. My mother has always been a drama queen, so I suspect Nicholas was telling the truth," she said solemnly.

"Too bad. It sounds like the guy deserved more than a black eye." Zach lowered his gaze, toying with her fingers before he looked back up at her. "Thank God your great-uncle came home in time. But the jerk still hurt you, didn't he." It wasn't really a question and Zach's green eyes were fierce.

"He grabbed me, held me down and tore my shirt. And he groped me so hard. I had bruises the next day."

Anger hardened the planes of Zach's face and a muscle flexed along his jawline. Without thinking, Cynthia reached out and stroked her fingertips over the vee between his brows, smoothing away the fierce frown.

"It was fairly traumatic for a twelve-year-old, but when I was at college I saw a counselor. She helped me come to terms with what happened."

He leaned in closer, resting his forehead against hers. "I'm so damn sorry, honey. No young girl should have to go through that and no woman should have to deal with the bad memories you must have had." He eased back, just far enough to look down and see her eyes. "Why did you wait until you were in college—why didn't you get counseling when it happened?"

"Natasha didn't have insurance and to be honest, I don't think she wanted her friends to know it happened."

Zach swore under his breath.

"It takes courage to face a problem and sign up for counseling," he told her. "I'm proud of you."

His words went straight to her heart. Her throat closed and her eyes misted. "That's very sweet of you."

"Sweet?" He scowled at her. "I'm not sweet."

"I think you are," she insisted.

"Huh." He smoothed his hand over her hair, his fingers curving behind her ear once more. He seemed fascinated by the texture. "I wish Brodie would get counseling," he said absently. "We'd probably have to tie him up to get him there though, and even then, he wouldn't talk."

"You're really worried about him, aren't you?" Cynthia said with sympathy.

"Yeah, I am." His fingers left her hair, his mouth curving downward. "After Mom died and Dad started drinking, life was pretty bad. All of us are screwed up, one way or another, and it's probably worse because Dad blamed us for Mom's accident so we all feel guilty, on some level."

"But he couldn't," Cynthia protested, shocked. "You were just little boys."

"It didn't matter—he blamed us." Zach shrugged. "Me, mostly. We were all playing in the creek but I was the one who dared her to grab the rope swing and jump." His gaze grew distant. "I'll never forget the sound of the rope snapping, or her head hitting the rock. It makes me sick to my stomach even now." He shook his head. "We all have bad memories of that day and every day that followed until we left Indian Springs—and that's why Brodie doesn't want to come back here. We survived childhood, but none of us got out undamaged—we're all carrying too much baggage. But Brodie..." Zach paused, his eyes shadowed. "Brodie's always been darker. He keeps more inside. His outlet has always been rodeo. He kept moving, always shooting for the next championship, riding the bull no one else had ever ridden." He shook his head. "Take that away and what's he got?"

"He still has you—and Cade and Eli," Cynthia said softly. "Didn't you tell me Brodie and Cade both loved the Triple C?"

Zach nodded, the curve of his mouth brooding.

"Then bring him home. If he can't have rodeo and that dream is gone, won't he need something to take its place? There's so much to be done here on the ranch. He'd be needed here. His life would have purpose."

He stared at her, as if turning over her words, studying them as he studied her features.

"How did you get to be so smart?" he asked softly.

"I didn't," she whispered. "I'm faking it."

He laughed. "And so blessedly stable. In a world full of crazy people, you may be the only normal person I know."

"Oh, I don't know about that," she said without thinking. "You have no idea how abnormal I really am."

His gaze sharpened. "Are you keeping secrets from me, Cynthia?"

She hadn't meant to tell him. Even as she opened her mouth, she didn't mean to tell him now. But somehow, she couldn't lie after he'd bared his heart about his childhood and his worry over his brother.

"I am."

He leaned nearer to whisper in her ear, his lips brushing against the sensitive lobe and making her shiver. "Tell me, honey."

She turned her head, ever so slightly, her own lips brushing against the faintly rough bristle of beard stubble on his cheek. "Promise you won't laugh at me?"

"I promise," he whispered back.

"I've never slept with anyone." She breathed the words, tensing with dread as she braced herself for his response.

He went perfectly still. Then he shifted mere inches

back so he could look into her eyes. "You've never slept with anyone," he repeated as if he was sure he hadn't heard her properly.

She shook her head sideways, a small negative movement of her head, while her gaze remained fastened on his.

"Soooooo." His deep voice drew out the word. "You're a virgin?"

She nodded, a brief confirmation.

"I'll be damned," he whispered, amazement in his voice. "How did that happen?"

She lifted an eyebrow in disbelief.

"Sorry." He shook his head in self-derision. "That was a dumb question. Of course I know how it happened—or more accurately, how it *didn't* happen. What I meant was you're smart and funny and beautiful so there must have been guys hanging around drooling over you. Ah." He stopped speaking, understanding flashing across his features. "The jerk terrified you. That transferred to all the guys who wanted to date you, right?"

"That's about it," she agreed.

"Even after the counseling?"

"I was better after college but by then…" She lifted her shoulders in a what-can-I-say shrug. "I'd waited too long. Every time I thought I'd met the guy who would be understanding, when and if I was ready to tell him, it didn't pan out. Frankly, it was embarrassing—not that I'm ignorant," she clarified, wanting him to understand. "Movies are fairly explicit so, visually speaking, I'm educated. But let's face it, watching is not the same as participating. So—" she drew a deep breath "—here I am, twenty-eight years old and barely been kissed," she ended in an attempt at humor.

"Hey, don't make fun of your situation," he told her, giving her a little shake. "I can see how it happened. But on the other hand, you must have kept on meeting a lot of lame men. I can't believe someone didn't sweep you off your feet and seduce you."

"I think I must be a hard sell at seduction," she told him solemnly. "In fact, I've been told I'm frigid."

He chuckled, his warm gaze moving over her face. "Honey, that's just not possible. You really have known a lot of idiots, haven't you?"

"Do you think so?"

"I know so," he said with such certainty that a little part of Cynthia sighed with relief.

"Where have you been all my life?" she teased. "If I'd known you, I wouldn't have had to kiss so many frogs."

"If I'd known you, I wouldn't have let any other men near you," he vowed. "And as for kissing…" He broke off, his gaze intent. "I can guarantee you wouldn't have needed to kiss any frogs."

He rose and caught her waist, lifting her easily to a seat on the edge of the marble-tiled counter. With her hands resting on his forearms, she was at eye level with him.

"I'm not sure what the protocol is here. I don't want you to think I'm like any of those jerks you've known in the past and I damn sure don't want to scare you. But I think I'm addicted to kissing you." His voice roughened as he spoke, his eyes darker green between half-lowered black lashes. "Cards on the table, Cynthia—I want you more than I've ever wanted a woman. But knowing you're a virgin puts a whole new slant on this. I don't want to screw up, so we'll take it slow, okay?"

"Okay," she murmured. There was something freeing about seeing Zach less than completely self-assured. It leveled the playing field—sort of. "Over the years, I've purposely started discussions with coworkers to get their opinions about anyone past the age of sixteen remaining a virgin. To be honest, their reactions made me cringe. Mostly, they laughed. I wasn't sure what I expected from you but…" She paused, tracing the line of his jaw with the tip of her index finger. "You were great. Thank you."

"Don't thank me," he growled. "I'm trying not to sling you over my shoulder and carry you off to bed. I can't even think about all the possibilities without breaking out in a sweat and my eyes crossing."

"For some reason, I find that incredibly arousing," she said, laughing when he frowned at her.

"Don't tease," he warned her. "I'm hanging on by a thread here."

"So, are you saying no more kissing?" She really, really hoped he wasn't giving up on the kissing. He wasn't the only one who was addicted.

"You want kissing?" He watched her carefully, his muscles flexing, bunching with tension under her fingers.

"Definitely."

"Good," he muttered, nudging her knees apart and stepping between them. He tugged her forward, snugging the vee of her thighs against his silver-buckled belt. "If I go too far, too fast, tell me."

She barely nodded before he cupped her face in his hands and covered her mouth with his.

He licked her bottom lip and she caught her breath, her lips parting as he fused their mouths together. Heat roared between them as she followed the teasing strokes of his tongue with hers. When he finally lifted his head to look down at her, arousal streaked color over the arch of his cheekbones. Her arms were wrapped around his neck, her body pressed tightly against his, her cheeks hot.

"I'm going to follow you home," he said, his voice harsh with need. "Because if I don't, we're going to end up in my bed. Before that happens, I want to be damned sure we both know what we're doing and that you're ready for it."

Cynthia grumbled, but he was adamant. A short hour later, she was in her own bed, alone, and Zach was gone.

She knew tonight marked a fundamental shift in their relationship. She'd lowered shields she'd had in place for seemingly forever, told him things she'd never told anyone else and he'd responded with a fierce protectiveness that made her feel cherished.

He really was sweet, she thought sleepily. Incredibly sexy, too, and the nice-guy-side of him she'd seen tonight only made him more attractive. Smiling, she bunched the pillow under her head and drifted off to sleep, the taste of Zach's kiss still on her lips.

Chapter Thirteen

Zach hardly slept at all. When he wasn't tossing and turning, he was lying awake, staring at the ceiling.

Cynthia's revelations had placed him squarely between a rock and a hard place. He wanted her so bad his teeth ached. Even when he was working nonstop on the Lodge, he'd been thinking about the day when he'd coax her into his bed and planning exactly how to make that happen.

Now he wasn't sure it *should* happen. He'd never slept with a virgin. Even as a teenager, he'd avoided girls that were looking for more than a good time. As an adult, he had no interest in marriage, the word *relationship* wasn't in his vocabulary and he'd made sure the women he dated knew that up front. He never led anyone on.

But with Cynthia, he hadn't been thinking at all.

Much as he hated to admit it, he'd taken one look at her and all the rules he'd insisted on with women in the past had been forgotten. He wanted her. Whatever it took to get her, he was ready and willing to do.

Until she told him she was a virgin.

And damn if that only made him want her more—except now, he had this feeling he should be protecting her.

There was no solution. He groaned, staring at the pattern of moonlight flickering across the ceiling above his bed. No matter what he did, he was in trouble.

And the hell of it was, he liked her. He liked being around her. He liked the way she laughed—and the way she made him laugh.

But he couldn't sleep with her and take her virginity if it was only sex he wanted. What kind of a complete jackass would that make him?

Yet the thought of her sleeping with someone else made him feel homicidal.

When he finally fell asleep just as the sun was coming up, he was no closer to answering any of the questions that had plagued him all night long.

Both Cynthia and Zach were wary on Monday, walking carefully around each other, weighing their words. By Tuesday, some of their natural caution had eased and when Cynthia returned home after work, she was filled with optimism about the future.

She barely noticed the blue car parked at the curb just outside her house, humming to herself as she opened the door and stepped into the entry hall.

But the luggage piled haphazardly on the polished wood floor stopped her in her tracks. There was no mistaking the bright red bags, nor the hot pink pashmina shawl tossed over the newel post at the staircase.

"Natasha?" she called.

"In the kitchen." Her mother's voice carried easily down the hallway to the entry.

Cynthia closed her eyes for a moment, drawing in a deep breath and mourning the loss of her plans for a peaceful evening before she slowly released her breath and walked toward the kitchen.

"When did you get in?" she asked, crossing to the stove to switch on the kettle.

"A couple of hours ago," her mother answered from her seat at the table. A carafe, coffee cup and a small plate with crumbs sat on one side, the newspaper spread out in front of her, folded back to the crossword puzzle. "You're home late. Where have you been?"

"At work." Cynthia took tea bags from the tin and dropped one into a cup, the tag dangling over the side.

Natasha brightened. "You've found a job already? That's good news." A small frown marked a vee between her eyebrows. "Wait—where can you be working in Indian Springs?"

"Zach Coulter is renovating the Lodge on his family's ranch. I'm helping with prep work and will manage it when it's open to the public."

"Trust you to land on your feet," Natasha said approvingly. "I was sure you would." She sipped coffee and smiled. "That changes the situation, and all for the better, I must say. I wasn't looking forward to staying in Indian Springs for long."

"I assume you've left…" Cynthia couldn't remember the name of her mother's latest man friend.

"Yes, I simply had no choice," Natasha declared. "He was impossible to live with and, as it turned out, not very well-off. He actually lives on a budget."

Cynthia hid a smile at the faint horror in her mother's voice. Behind her, the teakettle began to sing and she poured boiling water into her cup, setting the kettle back on the stove before carrying her tea to the table. "Lots of people do, Natasha. Live on budgets, I mean."

"Well, it's not for me," Natasha said, shaking her head with dismissal.

"Are you going to look for a job here in Indian Springs?" Cynthia asked. One of Natasha's few redeeming features was that she was an expert medical transcriptionist and whenever she was between lovers, never had difficulty finding employment.

"I'd rather not. I'd much rather settle in a larger town like Great Falls or Missoula." Her face brightened. "Or Denver. And now that you're working, you'll be able to loan me funds to tide me over for a few months while I find a job and an apartment."

"I'm sorry, Natasha, but I'm barely making enough at the Lodge to cover the bills here," Cynthia explained. "Renovating the property is prohibitively expensive and I agreed to accept a salary package with escalating increases down the road."

"Why on earth would you do that when you're a highly qualified professional who can make a competitive salary away from this town?" Natasha demanded, frowning at her.

"Because I like Indian Springs and I want to stay here for a while," Cynthia said simply.

For the next half hour, she listened to her mother

rail and complain about her choice of residence and employment, knowing Natasha would eventually run down. When she did, Cynthia picked up her empty mug and set it in the sink.

"I'm going to have a shower before finding something for dinner. I'll be down shortly."

Natasha nodded sulkily and returned to her crossword puzzle.

As Cynthia climbed the stairs and entered her room, stripping off her clothes and collecting clean pajamas from the bureau drawers, she almost wished she had enough cash to hand over to her mother. At the moment, losing the money seemed preferable to having Natasha as a roommate for the coming days or weeks before she moved on.

Over the next week, Cynthia was surprised as Natasha seemed to accept that she would remain in Indian Springs for the foreseeable future. Her mother even displayed an interest in Cynthia's days at work, which she'd never done before. Normally, the only interest her mother had in Cynthia's job was the amount of income it generated.

Now, when Cynthia came home, Natasha would linger at the house, sharing coffee, tea or a late supper with her and quizzing her about her work.

Natasha always went out around 9:00 p.m. however, telling Cynthia she was meeting friends. Cynthia was familiar with all the signs and she suspected her mother had hooked up with a new guy, but as long as Natasha was happy and not stirring up a big scene, Cynthia was happy. She didn't ask questions.

Just after noon on Friday, Cynthia left her office at the Lodge and went looking for Zach. She found him in an upstairs bedroom with a crew of two other men, sanding hardwood floors.

"Can I see you for a minute?" she called from the doorway.

"Sure." He joined her in the hall, wood dust whitening the knees of his jeans. "What's up?"

"I wondered if you'd like to join me for an interview. I have Jane Howard scheduled for one o'clock—she's the assistant chef at the Black Bear, remember?"

"I remember the food. It was great. But you haven't needed me for the other interviews, why this one?"

"Because the others were preliminary visits. If I'd called them back for second interviews, I would have wanted you there for the final decision. But I think Ms. Howard might be our girl, which is why I'd like you to sit in on this first interview."

"As long as you don't mind my showing up in work clothes." He glanced down, brushing wood dust from the front of his dark blue T-shirt. "This isn't exactly a three-piece suit."

"I don't care what you wear. I need your people-reading skills and your brain, not your fashion sense."

He laughed. "That's good, because I'm not sure I have any fashion sense."

"You look perfect just as you are." She hadn't meant the words to come out quite so filled with appreciation. When Zach's gaze sharpened, darkened, she knew he'd read into the few words exactly how much she liked the way he looked in the snug faded jeans and dark T-shirt. "I'd better go." She took several steps backward before spinning and hurrying down the stairs and back to her office. She had the distinct feeling that if they'd been alone, he would have followed her.

One of these days, she thought with a shiver, *neither of us is going to want to say stop.*

Jane Howard arrived for her appointment five minutes early.

"Excuse me."

The feminine voice caught Cynthia's attention, and she looked up from the file of invoices. The woman standing in the office doorway looked to be in her mid- to late-twenties. Long-legged and slim in a conservative blue suit, white blouse and navy pumps, she had curly strawberry-blond hair pulled back into a French braid that hung down her back. Delicate brows winged above thick-lashed moss-green eyes and her creamy, pale skin looked too fair to survive in the hot Montana sun.

"Hello." Cynthia stood, welcoming her with a smile. "You must be Jane Howard?"

"Yes." The woman stepped inside. "I hope I'm not too early." She gestured at the open file on the desk in front of Cynthia. "I can come back if I'm interrupting…?"

"Not at all. Come in." Cynthia waved her to a seat in front of the desk. "I'm Cynthia Deacon."

"It's a pleasure to meet you."

"Am I late?" Zach said from the door.

"Not at all." Cynthia saw Jane turn to look at Zach, but the other woman's face reflected only a polite inquiry. "This is Jane Howard—Jane, this is Zach Coulter, the owner of the Lodge."

"Nice to meet you, Jane—no, don't get up." He waved her back into her seat. "We're casual here. You'll have to forgive us if you'd expected a more formal grilling." He dropped into a heavy oak chair set at right angles to Cynthia's desk, facing both women.

Jane seemed to relax slightly at Zach's words. "Casual works for me," she said with a reserved smile.

"Thanks for coming out to talk to us on such short notice," Cynthia told her. "We're moving at warp speed, hoping to hold a soft opening within a few weeks."

Jane's eyes widened slightly. "I hadn't realized it would be so soon."

"Would that be a problem for you if the position were offered?" Cynthia queried, handing a copy of Jane's résumé to Zach.

"I don't believe so. My boss at the Black Bear has always been understanding," she replied. "He knows I've applied for the position and if I needed to give him less than three weeks' notice, I'm sure he'd understand."

Over the next half hour, Cynthia asked Jane about her work history, her training and detailed questions about her qualifications to run a kitchen where guests would expect gourmet meals. Zach interceded with the occasional request for clarification. Throughout the exchange, Jane remained calm and professional, fielding their questions with intelligent, thorough answers.

Cynthia was impressed with both Jane's demeanor and her résumé.

"I think you've answered all the questions I have," she told Jane. "Zach, do you have anything more?"

"I do." He shot her a quick smile before focusing on Jane. "I'm impressed by your references, Jane, and it's clear the people you've worked with think you have a bright future. But the Lodge will be catering to clients from all over the world, some of whom probably employ full-time personal chefs. Tell me how a girl with no formal training, who's never worked at a five-star restaurant in New York, Paris or Los Angeles, can compete with someone who has."

Jane's pause was barely discernible before she replied. "While it's true I don't have the credentials other more formally trained applicants may have, I grew up on a ranch not quite sixty miles from here. My mother was an amazing cook and she taught me to prepare just about every local food available. If you want the Lodge to have a menu that's unique, then you need someone who can provide that, and do it well. That's what I can bring to the kitchen that you can't get with a chef imported from New York City or Los Angeles."

Zach grinned, his white teeth flashing in approval. "Well said," he told her. "Next question—the Lodge will be open all year long. Although the person we hire will have set days off, we'll provide a three-bedroom apartment as part of the employment package because I want them to live on-site. Would that be a problem?"

"I'm a single parent with a six-year-old son," she replied. "It wouldn't be possible for me to live on-site unless I could make arrangements for child care while I work. I'm not sure how I would do that here on the Triple C, away from Indian Springs."

"What kind of arrangements do you have now?" Zach asked.

"I don't believe we're allowed to ask personal questions," Cynthia interjected, giving him a warning glance. She hadn't missed the way Jane's fingers had tightened where they curved over the arms of the wooden chair.

"I'm not asking her how old she is or if she's married," Zach said smoothly. "And you don't have to answer if you're not comfortable doing so, Jane."

"I don't have a problem with your questions, Mr. Coulter," she responded. "I can understand that the situation here at the Lodge is unique. Basically, my son's father isn't part of our lives and I have no relatives in the area. My little boy stays with a neighbor when he's not at school and I'm working. But that wouldn't be possible if we lived here at the Lodge."

"No," Zach agreed. "It wouldn't—and it wouldn't make sense for you to drive him to Indian Springs and have to pick him up after work, then drive back here." He frowned. "We'll have to give that some thought."

"Perhaps I should make it clear..." Jane's chin firmed, her eyes darkening. "Much as I would love the opportunity to become chef here at the Lodge, my son is my first priority."

"Of course." Zach nodded soberly, his gaze gentling over the woman. "I understand." He turned to Cynthia. "I believe that's all the questions I have. Anything you wanted to add?"

"No, I don't have any more questions." She rose and Jane stood also, collecting her purse. Cynthia leaned forward over the desk and the two women shook hands, a firm meeting of palms and fingers.

Zach escorted Jane out of the room, returning a few moments later to lift an eyebrow in silent query.

"I like her," Cynthia said firmly.

"So do I," Zach said, his gaze studying her. "I was impressed by her references. And I was really impressed by her determination to turn down the job if her son isn't well cared for. She won't get many career opportunities like this one and I'm dead certain she won't take it if we can't work out day care for her boy."

"I feel the same." Cynthia met his gaze. "I want to hire her."

His mouth quirked, the smile reaching his eyes. "Are you sure?"

"Yes," she said firmly.

"Then it's a done deal. Figure out a way to keep her little boy occupied while she's working and make her an offer." He turned to leave.

"Zach." Her voice stopped him. He looked over his shoulder at her. "Thank you."

He smiled, winked and left.

She knew Zach would have denied it, but she was convinced he'd given the single mother the job not only because of her references, but due to the strength of character and her unshakable determination to put her son's welfare first, before her own career. Cynthia couldn't help but be touched by his kindness.

Late that afternoon, once again Cynthia was clearing her desk long after the rest of the work crew had left for the night. She was just leaving her office, laptop and purse in her hands, when Zach intercepted her.

"Stay and have dinner with me tonight," he coaxed, tucking a tendril of loose hair behind her ear.

"I really should go home," she told him. "I have a stack of files I want to go through."

"You work too hard," he told her. "As your boss, I'm officially telling you to take the rest of the night off. Besides," he told her, "I'm testing out the fireplace tonight so if you insist on working, we can eat in front of the fire."

He pulled her into the kitchen, took her laptop, purse and files from her arms and set them on the countertop. He disappeared into the quarters off the kitchen and returned a moment later with a bright blue wool blanket tossed over one shoulder.

"We can raid the refrigerator—Mariah always brings home food from the café." He pulled open the door and started taking out bags and white cartons. "Come here." He crooked a forefinger at her.

When she walked across the kitchen and joined him, he handed her two bags and a square container. His own arms laden, he bumped his hip against the door and it swung closed behind him.

"Head for the lobby and we'll light the fire."

Cynthia went with him, unable to resist. She loved spending time with him and they had little time alone since the Lodge was filled with other workers during the day. Tonight, though, they were the only two people in the quiet Lodge.

They entered the big room and crossed the glossy wood floor to the huge river rock fireplace. Wood was stacked on the hearth, waiting to be lit. Zach set his armful of food carriers down on the low rock seating shelf and shook out the blanket, letting it drift to cover the floor.

"Have a seat," he invited, before turning to touch a match to the fire.

Cynthia sank to her knees on the blanket, the bright blue wool soft under her. "Are you sure we want to eat on this?" she asked doubtfully as she deposited the restaurant bags and cartons. "What if we spill something on it?"

"Don't worry about it." Zach took sofa pillows from one of the few pieces of furniture in the big room and stopped to switch on the radio. The antique console radio was beautifully restored and fully functional, with amazing speakers and sound. The strains of classic blues filled the room and Zach adjusted the volume to a low background before he rejoined her on the blanket.

"Here we are." He dropped the pillows, frowning at the collection of bags and cartons on the blanket. "Be right back."

He strode off to the kitchen, returning moments later with plates, utensils, napkins, two stemmed glasses and a bottle of wine.

"I think we're ready," he told her, dropping down beside her and stretching his long legs out on the blanket.

"Ready for what?" she asked, eyeing him through the screen of her lashes. He'd showered and changed after work, the clean black T-shirt tucked into the waistband of snug faded jeans, polished black cowboy boots on his feet. A silver-buckled belt threaded through the loops of his low-slung jeans. He looked incredibly male, heartstoppingly handsome, and she wanted to lean over and kiss him so badly her hand shook as she opened a carton.

"For whatever we want," he answered. The timber of his voice had changed, lowered, and her stomach muscles clenched in response.

She needed to slow things down, she thought. Maybe tonight was the night they would make love. But first, she needed time to unwind from a day filled with stress. Maybe Zach did, too.

"First, I want food," she told him. She peered into the carton she held and her smile brightened. "Mmm, Stroganoff."

She looked at him. "What have you got?"

Obediently, he flipped the lid open on a restaurant carton. "Lasagna," he said with a grin.

"Nice. What's in the rest of the containers?"

They spent the next hour feeding each other bites from the eclectic mix of food. Cynthia was delighted to find a flat box filled with pastries and small cakes. "You are so lucky to have a future sister-in-law who works in a café with a fabulous baker," she told him, closing her eyes in bliss as she tasted the coconut pie.

"And I know it," he told her with emphasis. "I've already warned Cade that he has to share all the food Mariah brings home. Just because they're getting married doesn't mean he gets first choice of the munchies."

They sampled food until they were full. Zach was just refilling their wineglasses when he paused, tilting his head to the side to listen.

"This is my favorite song." He put aside the bottle, took the glass from her hand and set it on the wood floor. "Dance with me." He stood, holding out his hand and when she placed her fingers in his, he lifted her easily to her feet.

She went happily into his arms, the low muted growl of a saxophone filling the lobby.

He pulled her close and they moved to the rhythm, their bodies perfectly attuned as they swayed to the music. The song ended but another started immediately and they stayed locked together.

Cynthia threaded her fingers into the thick, softness of his hair at his nape, her face tucked into the curve of his throat. She felt restless, achy, and the pressure of his chest against the tips of her breast wasn't enough. She wanted more.

She tipped her head back, just enough to press a kiss against the underside of his chin. His arms tightened around her, his body tensing beneath her touch. When she pressed closer, he responded by lifting her higher against him, fitting her more closely against his chest, hips and thighs.

He brushed kisses against her temple, her cheekbones, and when his mouth took hers, they stopped dancing, focused on the press of bodies and heated exchange of lips and tongues.

"Honey," he murmured long moments later. "Let's go to my apartment."

"Yes." The answer was simple, inevitable and Cynthia knew it was the right time, the right place and the right man.

His arms tightened, crushing her to him, before he bent and swung her into his arms. Cynthia wrapped her arms around his shoulders, her face against his throat as he strode swiftly down the lobby, through the darkened kitchen, and into the apartment in the back. She caught only a glimpse of the lamplit living room before they entered his bedroom and Zach released her legs, letting her slide slowly down his length until her feet reached the floor.

He cupped her face and kissed her, his mouth hot,

carnal. When he lifted his head, she was dizzy with a need that tightened her body and made her ache. He reached around her and lowered the zipper on her dress before closing his hands over her shoulders to slip his fingers under the material. He pushed it down her arms and torso, letting it fall to pool at her feet.

Zach went still, his gaze hot and intent as he stared at her. She wore a white lace bra and matching lace panties with a garter belt and hose; nerves tightened as she wondered with sudden uncertainty if he liked what he saw.

"Damn." His voice was guttural, barely audible. "You're more beautiful than I imagined." He glanced up at her. "And I've imagined you naked a lot."

"I'm not naked—yet." Her voice trembled, revealing nerves that shook as she tried to lighten the moment.

"Not yet, honey," he agreed with a slow curving of his lips. "But you will be."

He crossed his arms over his chest and caught the hem of his T-shirt, tugging it loose from his jeans and up over his head. It dropped to the floor behind him, ignored as Zach reached out and pulled her close, wrapping her against the bare, warm, hard muscles of his chest and abdomen.

Cynthia shivered, swamped with sensation.

Zach nudged her face up and kissed her again, his mouth hot and insistent on hers. She barely knew when he stripped off her bra, only aware of the feverish relief of her bare skin pressed to his. It wasn't until he lay her back on the bed and sat to pull off his boots, that the whirlpool of desire slowed and she was once again nervous. He leaned over and took a condom from a drawer in the nightstand, standing to shuck off his jeans, shove them, and his boxers, off with one smooth movement.

Cynthia caught her breath, staring at him.

"Something wrong?" His voice was deep, reassuring.

"Just…nervous," she said hesitantly.

"Trust me, Cynthia." His voice held amusement, along with lust and determination.

Then he rolled on the condom and joined her on the bed, his much bigger, harder, warmer body covering her. His mouth took hers and Cynthia was quickly lost in passion. So lost, that when he settled between her thighs, the heavy weight of him nudging insistently, she felt only impatience and urged him nearer.

Though he struggled to be slow, and careful, she didn't want easy and patient. She wrapped her legs around his waist and demanded—and he gave in. She fought to match his rhythm and at last, felt fierce delight when the world seemed to implode.

Long moments later, when she could catch her breath between labored gasps, she turned her head on the pillow to look at Zach.

"You," she told him with amazement, "are phenomenal."

He turned his head, his teeth flashing in the dim room. "You," he replied, "are amazing."

"We both are then," she said complacently.

"Are you okay?" He rolled over to face her, leaning his head on his hand, elbow propped on the pillow beside her head. "Sore anywhere?"

"I feel fabulous," she told him. "Women have been

losing their virginity for thousands of years and as far as I know, rarely have died from it."

"Jeez, I hope not," he said fervently.

She smiled. "In fact," she whispered, "I feel so good, I'd like to do it again."

"Now?"

"Yes, right now. Please," she added.

He roared with laughter and pulled her into his arms, rolling onto his back with her settling on his chest. "Honey, women can do it all night long, but men need a little recovery time."

"How long?" she asked, stroking her hand over his bare chest to his abdomen, fascinated by the faint line of silky dark hair that surrounded his navel before arrowing lower.

"You keep doing that and it probably won't be long," he told her drily.

And as it turned out, it wasn't very long at all.

They didn't sleep. In between lovemaking, they opened another bottle of wine and lay in front of the fire, talking about everything and nothing, the people they'd known, the places they'd traveled.

But morning came all too soon and just before dawn, Zach bundled her up and drove her home, insisting he didn't want her driving alone so early in the morning.

Despite protesting that she didn't need to sleep in, Cynthia obeyed Zach's orders and didn't wake till after 10:00 a.m. Carrying her coffee into the quiet living room on her way upstairs to the shower, she glanced out the front window and saw her car sitting at the curb.

Zach must have returned it this morning, she thought. How sweet.

She floated through the rest of the week in a daze. She'd always hoped making love would be a wonderful experience.

With Zach, she'd found it to be the most incredible, earthshaking thing she'd ever done.

Chapter Fourteen

Late Friday afternoon, Cynthia was tidying her desk, preparing to leave the office on time for a change. She and Zach had plans to have dinner and see a movie later that evening and she wanted time to do her nails and fix her hair before he picked her up.

She was slipping her laptop into its carrying case when Zach appeared in her open doorway. Her welcoming smile faded as she took in his grim expression.

"What's wrong?"

"I just got a call from the commissioner of the county zoning board. They're holding an emergency meeting an hour from now and asked me to be there. Someone's brought a complaint about the Lodge."

Cynthia's eyes widened. "A complaint? About what?"

"I don't know," Zach said grimly. "We've complied with all the local and state rules so I'm hoping it's just a question of proving we have all the right permits. But just in case, I'd like you to come with me and bring your file on zoning permits."

"Of course." Cynthia crossed to the filing cabinet and pulled open the middle drawer. "I can't help but wonder who would have filed a complaint," she said as she extracted a file folder and slid the drawer closed.

"I'd like to know that myself." Zach's mouth was a hard line. "I know it's bogus and we can prove we've complied with the rules, but if the process drags out for any reason, it's bound to impact the date for reopening the Lodge. And that has the potential to cost us a great deal of money and clients."

Cynthia knew he was right. Everything they'd done focused on the soft opening of the Lodge and its future hung in the balance. If the opening had to be delayed for any reason, the project's success would be in jeopardy.

"I'll follow you in my car and go straight home after the meeting," she told Zach.

He nodded and headed across the lot to his truck, long strides eating up the distance. By the time Cynthia had settled her files, laptop, purse and jacket into her car, he was driving down the lane.

They reached the meeting room in the county office building just as the four commissioners were settling into their seats. The long table faced two shorter tables with chairs pushed up to them and the bench seats that filled the rest of the room.

"Good evening," an older man on the right called. "You're Zach Coulter?"

"That's right."

"Will you come on down and take a seat at the table on the left, please?"

Zach and Cynthia walked down the aisle between the benches and took seats just as the door opened behind them.

Cynthia glanced over her shoulder. Jim Meyers walked toward the front of the room, his affable smile in place as he reached the front and took one of the chairs at the smaller table on the right.

"Good afternoon, gentlemen." He nodded at the commissioners. "And ladies," he added as he reached the fourth commissioner before his gaze moved to Cynthia and Zach. His nod was pleasant.

Cynthia didn't nod back. Tense with worry, she folded her hands on the table and struggled to appear calm. If Jim Meyers was involved in whatever was going on, it couldn't be good.

"I suggest we get right to business." The commissioner who had greeted them rapped a small gavel on the tabletop. "Thanks to everyone for being here on such short notice. This meeting is called to order. We're here for a preliminary hearing regarding certain information that has been brought to our attention about usage plans for the Coulter Lodge."

The older woman on the far right leaned forward, peering over the tops of her half-glasses at the commissioner. "Sorry to interrupt, Bill, but shouldn't we give a copy of the evidence to Mr. Coulter?"

"Thanks for reminding me, Hazel, of course we should." He slipped two stapled, multipage documents from a paper-clipped stack in front of him. "Mr. Coulter, if you and your associate would like to have a copy…"

Zach left the table to collect the papers from the commissioner, murmuring his thanks before returning to the table. He handed one of the two documents to Cynthia as he sat down.

"You will note that the documents are on Coulter Lodge letterhead and contain cost analyses and plans proposing the site be used for conferences with attendee numbers that are far in excess of that allowed by your current permits."

Cynthia flipped through the pages, confusion growing.

"Do you know anything about this?" Zach leaned closer, his voice a low rumble.

"Yes," she whispered. "This was a preliminary projection. It didn't meld with your plans for the Lodge so I never showed it to you and it never went any farther."

Zach sat back in his chair. "I think we can clear up the confusion, gentlemen. I'm told this document was prepared as a preliminary analysis and was never intended as a viable future project."

"But we've been told an organization with over a thousand members has been approached regarding booking their annual conference there in two years."

Zach's eyes narrowed. "You've been told? By who?"

"By me," Jim Meyers interjected. "Actually, as conference chair for the state developer's association, I was approached by Ms. Deacon during lunch at the Indian Springs Café some weeks ago and then later…" He drew a sheet of paper from the file on the table and handed it to across the aisle to Zach. "I received this letter from the Lodge repeating the interest in booking my organization."

Zach skimmed the letter before handing it to Cynthia.

She read it quickly, then reread, frowning. "I've never seen this before. I certainly didn't write it."

"How did you receive this, Meyers?" Zach asked, his deep voice lethal. "Postal service or email?"

The other man blinked, pausing for a moment before responding. "Postal service—at my office."

"Do you have the envelope it arrived in that shows the post office marks?"

"No." Meyers's shrug held regret, but his eyes were sharp with satisfaction. "I'm afraid I tossed it out."

"Naturally," Zach commented. He turned back to the four commissioners, who watched the byplay with interest. "There's clearly a misunderstanding here that needs clearing up, but let me assure the board we will do so."

The bulky gray-haired man holding the gavel gave an abrupt nod. "Good. We'd like to see this resolved, too. But in the interim, we have no choice but to suspend your operating permit for the Lodge until you can provide an explanation. The board doesn't want to be placed in a position down the road of seeming to sanction an expansion of the creek bank usage at the Lodge. Environmental protection rules are strict and those federal boys are hardcore about enforcing them."

"I understand," Zach assured him. "I suggest we meet back here on Monday afternoon for an update."

"Think you can untangle the wires and iron out this mess that fast?" Bill asked, blue eyes shrewd.

"I hope so," Zach said shortly.

"Very well." Bill rapped the gavel on the table. "Meeting adjourned until 4:00 p.m. on Monday."

Chairs scraped back as the commissioners rose, gathered files and chatted among themselves. Jim Meyers stood and strolled forward to join them, asking a question about an upcoming meeting and revising a certain zoning requirement.

Zach turned to Cynthia, his back to the room, effectively blocking her and preventing anyone from overhearing him.

"Did you have anything to do with this, Cynthia?" His tone was impersonal.

"Of course not," she protested. "I have no idea how this happened."

"Did you talk to Meyers about the Lodge?" His green eyes were intent, cool as they focused on hers.

"*He* approached *me* at the café," she said forcefully. "He asked me to set up a meeting with you to discuss his buying the Lodge. I refused to do it."

"How did he get those projections?"

"I don't know," she said helplessly. "The files are on my laptop, but I always carry it with me, either at home or the office. I can't imagine how he did it."

"And the letter?" Zach asked, his tone businesslike, cool.

She shook her head. "I don't know, Zach. I truly don't know."

"All right." He stood, waiting for her to walk ahead of him out of the room. He was silent as they left the building.

She paused on the sidewalk, looking up at him. "What are you going to do?"

"Find out how this happened. I'm sure Meyers is behind it, but I can't prove it until I find out how he did it." He tugged the brim of his Stetson lower over his brow, his eyes concealed behind the mirrored lenses of his sunglasses. "I won't be able to make dinner tonight. This is likely to take all weekend so I probably won't see you until Monday."

"What can I do to help?"

"Nothing. I don't want you involved in this. Take the weekend off and I'll see you Monday."

"All right." Cynthia felt sick. His words were even, with an undercurrent of anger and no hint of the warmth that usually infused his conversation with her.

He nodded and walked away, headed for the slot where he'd parked his truck down the street. Cynthia turned, moving the opposite direction toward her own car, when someone walked up behind her.

"I told you, you'd be sorry," Meyers murmured as he slowed to brush past her, then picked up his steps to move more quickly down the sidewalk.

Furious with the implication of what had happened in the meeting room, Cynthia registered the malicious satisfaction in his words.

She could easily believe Jim Meyers was vindictive enough to want to pay her back for having turned down his request to set up a meeting with Zach. In retrospect, she thought as she drove toward home, it was precisely the sort of thing she should have expected of him.

What she couldn't understand was how he'd gotten the documents off her computer. The only place the documents were stored were on her laptop and the external, backup hard drive in her bedroom at home. Jim Meyers didn't have access to either storage so how on earth had he managed to get his hands on those documents?

He could easily have generated the letter and forged her signature, but again how had he accessed the Lodge letterhead? By the time she climbed into bed later that evening, a full-blown headache pounded at Cynthia's temples. But she was no closer to answers to the questions that plagued her.

Zach left Indian Springs and drove back to the Triple C in a cold rage. The urge to grab Meyers and torture him until he confessed the truth was a ball of acid in Zach's gut.

He knew he was in no mood to be reasonable. Meyers's insistence that Cynthia had given him the information that had led to the Lodge's permit being suspended couldn't be true. He refused to believe she would have sold him out and threatened the survival of the Lodge.

But the cynic that lived inside him laughed with derision. If his years as a corporate shark had taught him anything, it was that everyone had their price. What if Meyers had offered Cynthia something she couldn't refuse—like part-ownership in one of his company's land deals?

The idea was ludicrous. Even as Zach thought it, he knew it couldn't be true. But Meyers's claim that Cynthia had betrayed Zach was insidious, and doubt refused to evaporate, taunting him with the possibility that the woman he loved had betrayed him.

What the hell?

Where did that come from? He thought, dumbstruck. When had he decided he loved Cynthia?

The truck slowed and he realized he'd lifted his foot off the accelerator. He forced himself to focus on driving again, but the biggest portion of his mind was occupied with accepting the truth he'd hidden, even from himself.

He loved Cynthia. He didn't know the exact moment it happened. Was it the first time he'd seen her on the street in Indian Springs? Or the first time he'd kissed her? The second time? The night she'd told him she was a virgin?

Zach shook his head, dazed. He didn't know when it had happened, but he knew without doubt it was true.

Did she love him? He frowned. He knew she liked making love with him, and for a woman who'd kept her virginity for so long that had to mean something. He wanted to turn the truck around and drive straight to her house to find out how she felt about him.

He actually braked before he caught himself. Before they could have that conversation, he needed to clear up the mess Meyers had stirred up.

He was furious that the land developer was trying to harm the Lodge, and that he'd also try to damage Cynthia's reputation.

Nevertheless, he knew using physical force would only play into Meyers's hands. Zach had to figure out how he'd managed to access Cynthia's computer records without her knowledge.

And if I can prove he broke in and stole information, I'm going straight to the cops and have him arrested, he thought grimly.

He arrived at the ranch and drove to Mariah's cabin, parked outside and rapped on the door.

"Where's Cade?" he asked when Mariah opened the door.

"In the kitchen. What's wrong?" she called after him as he strode past her and down the hall.

Cade was standing at the counter, replacing screws in one of the original wooden cabinet doors. He looked over his shoulder when Zach entered.

"What's going on, Zach?"

"What do you know about Jim Meyers? I want to nail his hide to the barn," Zach said grimly, anger making his voice harsh.

Cade left the cabinet unfinished, leaned against the counter, crossed his arms over his chest, and eyed Zach.

"Tell me what he's done."

Zach quickly filled Cade in on the meeting with the commissioners.

"And Meyers said Cynthia gave him the information?" Cade asked.

"I don't believe it," Mariah put in. "I saw Jim Meyers approach Cynthia at the café one day during lunch. But she didn't look nor act as if she wanted to see him. Or talk to him for that matter," she added.

"I think he set her up, but I'm damned if I know how he did it," Zach growled, frustrated.

"Then we'll have to figure it out," Cade told him calmly, although his eyes were hard. "Who else besides Cynthia had access to the information?"

"She says nobody," Zach said. "But there must have been someone."

"One of the contractors? Or one of the suppliers for the Lodge?" Mariah asked.

"We'd better write down names," Zach told her. "My laptop's up at the Lodge—have you got paper and pens?"

Mariah hurried out of the room, and Zach looked at Cade.

"I'm not sleeping until I know how Meyers did this," he vowed grimly. "And when I find out, I'm going after him."

He didn't say it aloud, but he knew he wouldn't rest until Cynthia's name was cleared and she was safe.

Then he could ask her to marry him.

He refused to contemplate her saying anything but yes.

Cynthia spent the weekend trying to stay busy. She cleaned the house in a whirlwind of activity and late Sunday afternoon, when she could find nothing left that needed washing or polishing, she moved outdoors.

She raked the nearly spotless flower beds, fertilized the roses, shoveled and spread bark mulch beneath the trees and shrubs. She was inspecting the leaves on the lilac bushes for any brown spots when Natasha strolled out onto the porch.

"What on earth is wrong with you?" her mother asked as she settled into a wicker rocker, a glass of iced tea in one hand, a glossy fashion magazine in the other. "You've barely sat down all weekend and I swear, I don't think I've heard you say twenty words."

"Sorry, Natasha," Cynthia murmured, considering a

lilac leaf with a small blemish. Deciding not to remove it, she moved on to the yellow Peace rose next to it.

"What does that mean? You're sorry about what—not talking or not sitting still for two days?"

The faint echo of concern in Natasha's voice caught Cynthia's attention and she looked up, past the porch railing and at the chair where her mother sat.

"I suppose about not talking. I didn't realize I was being so uncommunicative."

"Yes, well…" Natasha waved the magazine impatiently. "You are. And although you're not exactly a chatterbox, you're rarely nearly silent, either. What on earth is wrong?"

Cynthia sighed, frowning at the rose leaf. "There's a…situation at work. I can't get my mind off it—I suppose that's why I haven't been very good company."

"What kind of a situation?" Natasha frowned. "Not more bad boss problems?"

"No." Cynthia shook her head in instant denial. "Not at all. Zach's a great boss."

"Then what's the problem?" Natasha insisted, sipping her tea.

"Someone made a complaint to the zoning commission about the permits for the Lodge."

"Someone? Who was it?"

"I don't think I should say more until Zach gives me permission to talk about it." Cynthia realized she'd gripped the green leaf so tightly that it had torn in two.

"Well, if you ask me," Natasha said with a sniff. "It sounds like much ado about nothing. The Coulters have enough influence to do whatever they want with the Lodge. Who could stop them?"

"The zoning commission has the power to rescind permits and block the opening," Cynthia told her.

"I've heard rumors that Zach plans to open the Lodge and when it becomes popular, sell it and go back to California. Is that true?"

"I don't know." Cynthia wished she knew what Zach's plans were, but he seemed totally focused on the opening date and hadn't said anything definitive beyond that time.

"If he's not going to stay, it would be better if he sold," Natasha commented. "Businesses are healthier with a local owner. Absentee owners are always bad for business."

Cynthia stared at her mother. "I heard someone else say almost the same thing not so long ago," she said slowly. "Have you been talking to Jim Meyers, Mother?"

Faint pink color tinted Natasha's cheeks. "What if I have?" she asked defensively. "Why shouldn't I?"

"No reason. I wasn't aware you knew him."

Natasha leaned over and set her tea glass down on the low wicker table, her gaze averted. "I ran into him at the pharmacy when I first arrived."

"Are you seeing him?" Cynthia held her breath, hoping against hope the answer was no.

"We've gone out." Natasha shot Cynthia a defensive glare. "I know he's younger than me, but he's a lot of fun. There's nothing wrong with dating a younger man."

"Of course not," Cynthia said patiently. "But he's the one who made the complaint to the zoning commission about the Lodge. He had access to information that he shouldn't have."

Natasha looked startled, then angry. "He's never asked me anything about the Lodge—and it's not as if I know anything I could have told him anyway. You don't tell me anything about your work except generalities."

"No, I don't." Her mother was right. She didn't talk about confidential work matters with anyone but Zach, so Meyers couldn't have gotten his information from Natasha. She sighed and tugged off her gloves, abandoning the rosebush to climb the porch steps. "But he seems to have a questionable character, Natasha. I hope you don't get involved with him."

"I'm not involved. I told you, we enjoy each other's company. That's all."

Cynthia sincerely hoped her mother was telling the truth. Because Jim Meyers had shown a nasty, vindictive side that she hoped wouldn't impact Natasha. "I think I'll go in and take a shower to wash away the garden dirt, then start dinner. Will you be here or are you going out?"

"I'm meeting friends at the Black Bear this evening for dinner, then we're going on to catch a movie."

"Sounds like fun." Cynthia pulled open the screen door. "I'll be down in a bit." She stepped inside and heard her mother murmur she'd see her later as she crossed the entryway and headed upstairs.

As she showered and shampooed her hair, she tried to decide if she should call Zach and tell him Natasha had been dating Jim Meyers. She'd definitely gotten the impression Zach wanted her out of the way, and uninvolved, while he did what was necessary to find out how Jim had managed to get the file.

Face it, she told herself with brutal honesty, *Zach probably thinks you gave Jim Meyers that information.*

She felt sick every time she thought about it. She was the only person who'd had the information in her possession. She had no explanation for how Meyers had managed to gain access to it—and certainly no evidence that could prove she was innocent of aiding him.

If she were Zach, she would be able to draw only one conclusion—all the evidence pointed to her guilt.

Her stomach was tied in knots, but by the time she'd dried her hair, then dressed in clean shorts and a top, she'd made up her mind. She picked up her cell phone and dialed Zach.

"Hello." The familiarity of his deep voice was both comforting and fraught with tension for Cynthia.

"Hi, Zach, it's me."

"Cynthia, what's up?"

At least he didn't sound angry and he hadn't immediately hung up, she thought. "I have some information for you, although I don't know if it will help or just make things more confusing."

"What is it?" He sounded interested but faintly distracted, as if his attention was elsewhere.

"My mother has been seeing Jim Meyers."

Silence met her statement.

"Zach? Did you hear me?"

"Yeah, I heard. Since when?"

"She said they ran into each other shortly after she came back to town, so it's been a few weeks." Cynthia wished she could tell if he thought the information was helpful. "I don't see how this helps but I thought I should tell you. It just seems suspicious that he's seeing my mother at the same time he somehow gained possession of documents he could only have accessed off my computer."

"Sounds too coincidental—unbelievably so," Zach agreed. "Didn't you tell me you have an external hard drive at home that you use to back up your laptop files?"

"Yes, I do. But it's password protected. I don't see how he could have gained access."

"Hold on." His voice was instantly muffled, as if he'd covered the receiver with his hand. "Are you going to be home for a while?"

"Of course."

"I'm sending J.T. in to pick up your hard drive and laptop. Are you okay with that?"

"Certainly. But I'd be glad to bring it out if you need it, Zach."

"No." His voice was adamant, brusque. "I don't want you involved in this. J.T. will be there in about twenty minutes or so—I'll need passwords for your locked files on the laptop and access to the external drive."

Cynthia gave him the information and a moment later, he said goodbye.

A little while later, J.T. knocked on her door, collected the laptop and hard drive and after a few moments left, but since the teenager had known as little as Cynthia about what Zach was up to, she was none the wiser.

Anxious to know whether Zach had solved the mystery, Cynthia arrived at work early the following morning, only to learn that Zach wasn't there.

When he hadn't shown up by noon, she called Cade.

"I was hoping to talk to Zach this morning," she told him. "Do you know where he is?"

"He drove down to Billings to pick up a visitor at the airport. He wants you to meet him at the commissioners' offices at four this afternoon."

And that was all the information Cade would give her. She was sure he knew more about the mysterious visitor and Zach's investigation, but if he did, he wasn't sharing.

Frustrated, Cynthia went back to work, checking shipping invoices against the deliveries by hand. Her laptop still hadn't been returned.

The afternoon dragged. By the time she arrived at the commissioners' offices, she was strung tight with nerves. Cade and Mariah pulled in behind her and the three walked in together, taking a seat on the bench just behind the tables.

Within a few moments, Jim Meyers entered the room. He sat on the opposite side of the aisle, in the same row.

Cynthia kept glancing at her watch.

"What's keeping Zach?" she whispered to Mariah.

"Cade says he'll be here, don't worry," Mariah whispered back.

The door to the commissioners' chambers opened and the three men and Hazel filed in. All of them greeted Mariah, asking her how things were at the café.

Just as the commissioners were taking seats and opening files, the door at the rear of the room opened. Cynthia twisted to look behind her and saw Zach holding the door to let two women enter the room ahead of him.

One was a stranger, a young woman with center-parted, straight black hair that fell to her hips in a shining ebony fall. Black kohl eyeliner accented eyes that were a deep turquoise; her skin was so fair it seemed almost white, and scarlet lipstick accented her full lips. She was dressed all in black and when she turned her head to say something to Zach, her hair swung back over her shoulder, revealing multiple gold studs and hoop earrings along the rim of her ear. A smocked top fell to mid-thigh over black leggings and black leather boots reached almost to her knees.

She looked as alien as if a spaceship had dropped her onto Indian Springs's Main Street.

And when Zach bent his head to listen to her, the intimacy between the two was obvious. A sharp, suffocating pain caught Cynthia and for a moment, she couldn't breathe.

Then the woman stepped away from Zach and walked down the aisle. For the first time, Cynthia looked at the other woman and realized it was Natasha.

Zach followed the two women down the aisle, setting Cynthia's laptop and external drive on the small table in front. The younger woman pulled out a chair and sat at the table, while Zach ushered Natasha to a seat next to Cynthia.

Their eyes met, caught, and he winked before turning away to the table.

Cynthia drew a deep, shuddering breath, reassured by his glance. Before she could ask her mother what was happening, however, the commissioner rapped the gavel.

Cynthia heard the soft sound of the exit door opening and closing, the sound nearly covered by the gavel. She glanced over her shoulder to see a sheriff's deputy had entered and now sat in the last bench before the exit.

"Mr. Coulter," the commissioner said.

Cynthia faced front once again, riveted by the unfolding drama.

"It appears you may have some information to present to the commission?" he asked.

"Yes, I do." Zach stood. "I believe I've solved the mystery as to how preliminary documents, which were never more than one of many possibilities for the Lodge's future and never intended for the Lodge to pursue, were stolen from Cynthia Deacon's computer." He turned to the black-haired woman. "This is my assistant, Angela Freewater. She's a computer expert, and I asked her to run some tests on Ms. Deacon's computer and external hard drive where she backs up all her work. I believe you'll find her comments interesting."

Angela stood as Zach sat. In a smooth, laconic drawl, she gave the enthralled listeners a ten-minute lesson on tracking cyber crime. Then she explained how she'd accessed Cynthia's computer and backup drive, run scans that traced the accessing of both, and identified the hacker who'd done it.

"And who was it?" Zach asked.

"The hacker's name is Jim Meyers."

Across the aisle from Cynthia, Meyers shot to his feet. "That's a lie," he blustered. "It's impossible for anyone to do what she says she did. I'm being set up."

"It's not impossible when the hacker is an amateur who uses his own laptop to hook up to an external drive," Angela said with barely a hint of contempt. "And his laptop leaves fingerprints any ten-year-old computer geek can read, trace and identify."

Meyers's face turned red and he looked apoplectic.

Zach stood once more and Angela took her seat.

"We also have a witness who can corroborate that Meyers had access to Cynthia's house where she kept the backup hard drive, and that he had sufficient time to download the information."

He turned, gesturing to Natasha, who stood.

Cynthia had never seen her mother so angry. Her eyes shot sparks as she glared across the aisle at Meyers.

"I can verify that Mr. Meyers had access to our house—and that he abused our trust and apparently, is little better than a cheat and a scoundrel," she said dramatically.

Cynthia had never before been glad her mother was a drama queen but for this moment, she was profoundly thankful.

The commissioners were clearly impressed—even the lone woman, Hazel, nodded and looked at Jim Meyers as if he'd just crawled out from under a rock.

"Thank you, Natasha," Zach said, stepping back to take her arm and seat her once again, his solicitous gesture earned him a regal nod.

Cynthia caught the swift glance he shot her, and saw the amused gleam in his green eyes.

"I think that unravels the tangled threads," Zach told the commissioners. "Except for one final thing." He gestured over his shoulder. "I've filed a formal complaint with the sheriff's office and a deputy is here to arrest Mr. Meyers for theft. I'm also consulting with my attorneys as to possible civil action to sue Mr. Meyers for conspiracy to damage the reputation of Ms. Deacon and the financial standing of the Lodge."

"Now, look here," Meyers said, his voice loud, his face growing even redder. "This is ridiculous. I haven't done anything illegal."

"That's up to the judge to decide, Meyers," Zach shot back.

The deputy led Meyers away in handcuffs, the door closing on his shouts of protest.

"I believe that concludes our business," Bill the commissioner announced. "Mr. Coulter, your permit to operate is no longer suspended. I hope you'll invite us all to your opening."

"I'd be disappointed if you aren't there," Zach reassured him.

"Glad to hear it. We stand adjourned." The sound of the gavel hitting the table was loud.

Everyone stood, milling about as the commissioners exited.

Cynthia turned to her mother. "Natasha, thank you for coming down here today."

"Not a problem," her mother assured her, still clearly incensed. "Can you imagine that worm of a man, leaving my bed to go sneak into your room and hack into your computer?"

Cynthia blinked. "You were sleeping with him?"

"Only a few times." Natasha waved her hand dismissively. "He wasn't impressive."

Cynthia looked over her shoulder and realized Zach

had heard every word of their conversation. She closed her eyes, wincing, but when she quickly opened them, he was grinning at her.

"We're all going out to dinner," Cade said behind her. "How about the Black Bear Restaurant?"

"That sounds great." Zach sidestepped Natasha, wrapped his arm around Cynthia's waist, and with smooth precision, extricated her from the group. "We'll meet you there," he called over his shoulder as he hustled Cynthia out into the hall.

"Where are we…" She stopped talking when Zach pushed open an exit door and pulled her into a stairwell. Alone in the silent enclosed area, he backed her against the wall and kissed her.

His mouth was impatient, eager, his body pinning her against the wall and holding her there with gentle force. Cynthia welcomed the hard crush of his arms and the demand of his mouth on hers. She wrapped her arms around his neck and kissed him back. When at last he lifted his head, she was breathless and aroused.

"Why didn't you tell me Angela could find out what happened to my computer?" she demanded, tugging on his hair.

"Ow." He winced. "Because I wasn't absolutely sure she could when I sent J.T. in to get it."

"How did she do it so fast?"

"I hooked the external drive up to your laptop, hooked the laptop up to the internet, and gave Angela your passwords. She did it all through cyberspace."

"Wow." Cynthia was impressed. "She really is a computer genius, isn't she?"

"That she is," Zach agreed, sliding his hands beneath her knit top to stroke her midriff. "How hungry are you?" he muttered moments later, after both of them were breathing too fast, their lips damp from the kiss just ended.

"I'm hungrier for you than I am for food," Cynthia murmured, brushing her lips over the underside of his chin.

"Good," he managed to say, his voice rasping. "Let's go home."

"Home?" She leaned back to look up at him. "My place or yours?"

"My place— I'd choose your place since it's so much closer, but your mother might come home and interrupt us. And I don't plan to let you go until morning."

She smiled, a slow curving of her lips that she was sure gave away how much she was looking forward to spending the night with him.

"Have I ever told you how much I love you?" she murmured.

She felt his muscles go taut, his arms tightening around her and his gaze searched hers.

"No." His voice was gravelly, rough with emotion. "You haven't. And I need to hear you say it again."

"I love you," she whispered, tears welling to roll slowly down her cheeks.

"When did you know?" he asked, the pad of his thumb smoothing over her cheek, gently brushing away the dampness.

"I think I knew for sure when Jim Meyers said I'd given him information to harm the Lodge. I was devastated that you would think I'd betray you." She searched his eyes. "I would never do anything to harm you, Zach."

"I know." He bent to trace her trembling lips with his. "I was mad as hell, but it took about ten minutes to realize there's no way you could have done what he claimed you did. That's when I realized I was in love with you."

"Thank goodness," she breathed. "I was so afraid you'd go back to San Francisco and leave me here alone. It's scary to love someone this much—you could break my heart."

"Not tonight," he whispered back. "Not ever."

"I love you lots." She smiled against his throat when she felt his pulse jump.

"Not as much as I love you," he growled, his voice rumbling in his chest.

"Is this a contest?" she asked.

"No, but if it is, we're both going to win," he said gravely, his green gaze meeting hers with sober intent. "Let's go home so I can propose in a place that has a bed nearby."

Cynthia felt her eyes widen. "You're going to propose?" she murmured, her voice faint.

"I was thinking about it. Think you'll say yes?" he asked.

"Oh, I think that's a definite possibility," she replied.

Zach's eyes flared with green fire and as his mouth covered hers, Cynthia hazily realized that she held everything she'd waited for, for so long, here in his arms.

* * * * *

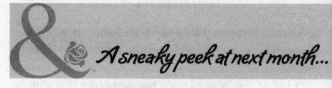

A sneaky peek at next month...

Cherish™

ROMANCE TO MELT THE HEART EVERY TIME

My wish list for next month's titles...

In stores from 16th November 2012:

❏ The Count's Christmas Baby – Rebecca Winters

& The Rancher's Unexpected Family – Myrna Mackenzie

❏ Snowed in at the Ranch – Cara Colter

& The Nanny Who Saved Christmas – Michelle Douglas

In stores from 7th December 2012:

❏ The English Lord's Secret Son – Margaret Way

& A Gift for All Seasons – Karen Templeton

❏ A Maverick for the Holidays – Leanne Banks

& A Maverick's Christmas Homecoming – Teresa Southwick

Available at WHSmith, Tesco, Asda, Eason, Amazon and Apple

Just can't wait?

MILLS & BOON® Book Club

2 Free Books!

Get your free books now at
www.millsandboon.co.uk/freebookoffer

---

r fill in the form below and post it back to us

E MILLS & BOON® BOOK CLUB™—HERE'S HOW IT WORKS: Accepting your e books places you under no obligation to buy anything. You may keep the books d return the despatch note marked 'Cancel'. If we do not hear from you, about a nth later we'll send you 5 brand-new stories from the Cherish™ series, including 2-in-1 books priced at £5.49 each, and a single book priced at £3.49*. There is extra charge for post and packaging. You may cancel at any time, otherwise we send you 5 stories a month which you may purchase or return to us—the choice ours. *Terms and prices subject to change without notice. Offer valid in UK only. plicants must be 18 or over. Offer expires 31st January 2013. **For full terms and nditions, please go to www.millsandboon.co.uk/freebookoffer**

s/Miss/Ms/Mr (please circle)
_____

st Name
_____

rname
_____

ldress
_____

_____

_____ Postcode

mail
_____

end this completed page to: Mills & Boon Book Club, Free Book ffer, FREEPOST NAT 10298, Richmond, Surrey, TW9 1BR

Find out more at
www.millsandboon.co.uk/freebookoffer

Visit us Online

0712/S2YEA

Have Your Say

You've just finished your book.
So what did you think?

We'd love to hear your thoughts on our
'Have your say' online panel
www.millsandboon.co.uk/haveyoursa

- 🌹 Easy to use
- 🌹 Short questionnaire
- 🌹 Chance to win Mills & Boon® goodies